GIORDANO FALCO

THE SCIENTISTS
of
SOUTH BEND

Youcanprint

Titolo | THE SCIENTISTS of SOUTH BEND

Autore | GIORDANO FALCO

ISBN | 978-88-31615-74-7

Youcanprint
Via Marco Biagi 6 - 73100 Lecce
www.youcanprint.it
info@youcanprint.it

Introduction

The professor of applied physics Alan Adams during an experiment in which he amuses himself, along with five university colleagues, discovers the possibility to move items from one point to another instantly, with a tunnel created between two synchronized stations. This discovery could lead to a revolution in the transportation sector: no more trains, airplanes and cars, as well as in the tourism sector. The moment in which Adams realizes the significance of this finding, he rushes to warn his five colleagues and also his former teacher, Professor Tony Ross.

But his five colleagues are nowhere to be found.

One after the other they are kidnapped and an organization set up by an shady individual is getting ready to kidnap him too. Coincidentally, Alan avoids the kidnapping and begins to understand what's going on, he goes to the bank to withdraw money but the accounts are empty. At this point begins a flight through the U.S. during which the doctor, along with his girlfriend Sara Dixon, will escape ambushes and attempted murders until the final epilogue.

Translate by Isabella Cultrera

Chapter 1

MONDAY

Class was over and Professor Alan Adams gathered all his papers and documents he used for this lecture on applied physics from his desk at the Notre Dame University of South Bend in Indiana, and put them inside his leather handbag, scratched his beard and walked towards the exit, he was eager to get home and lock himself inside the laboratory to continue working on the experiment he had begun that same morning before leaving for class. He had to finish before evening because in two days time his colleagues would be back and they'd work on it together.

The variant of the equation proved by Alan that morning was a change to the original project that the others new nothing about yet; the night before he had had an intuition before falling asleep, he had brooded long over it while tossing and turning the whole night, and by 4 am he decided that staying in bed was useless, so he got up, made himself some coffee, lit on a Tuscan cigar and after having gone downstairs into the underground rooms of the laboratory he had begun the experiment with the variant that had tormented him the whole night; he had left the computer on to process the equation and now he was looking forward to see the results obtained.

He has started to smoke the cigar during his service in the Marines while in Italy, he had entered the Marine Corps and after a long and hard training he has been transferred to the Military Police, one night he had gone out with a comrade and two girls, his friend had invited him to try the Tuscan cigar, taught him to enjoy it without haste along with an aged brandy and he never parted from it since that night.

During his stay in Italy he had learned also all about good cuisine, the espresso coffee, good food and wine; the

Tuscan cigars were sent to him directly from Italy since it was hard to find them in the States.

He walked towards the exit door holding the briefcase in one arm, and just around the corner he saw Sara's slim figure walking towards him holding two cups of coffee.

– Hi Alan, I brought you some coffee– she said.

Sara Dixon was one of the math teachers and had had a crush on him since ever, Alan knew it and he was not insensitive to her charm either, they had become lovers, but he was not ready for a stable relationship with another woman: since his wife Anna died all he did was focus on his work and he avoided any kind of possible distraction that could then turn into anything serious, especially at night, he felt his wife's absence even more, when he used the microwave to cook his frozen meals and he could not but think of all the dishes she made him, he missed her terribly.

Their marriage had been full of love, they met in college and liked each other right from the start, but life's event separated them immediately, Alan's parents died in a car crash and he had to drop of out college to find a job and he choose the Military life.

Then he was forced to take leave, went back to study by getting scholarships and also thanks to the aid of an uncle who helped him out financially, they found each other again at University, and what they had postponed back in college now exploded stronger than ever, they saw each other again and fell in love, they married after one year without finishing their studies but a year later Anna died.

Anna came from an American Middle East peasant family, her parents had a farm near Plymouth in Indiana, they mainly cultivated corn, they had cows, hens and pigs.

Anna was an only daughter and since childhood she had not disdained the work in the fields, she drove the tractor and other agricultural vehicles like a man, but she had a predisposition for Humanistic studies and for art in general; She was an ironic person and was always fooling around with a veil of thin melancholy which was shown through her bright eyes. After attending the local college, she had enrolled at the faculty of Literature and while attending campus she had seen Alan again.

When they went to visit her parents in Plymouth, Alan felt at home, since his family was gone, he had adopted hers.

He liked the peace at the farm, the boundless spaces and even the smell of the freshly cut grass that pervaded the air; He had grown up in a popular neighborhood, respectable but very crowded, where the dominant smells were those of lamb cabbage or French fries, his father was a worker and his mother was housewife, so their finances were not very good.

His father had made huge sacrifices to send him to college, then they died and for Alan began a very hard period, he worked and studied at the same time, he regularly took scholarships, but life was not easy, so he tried an alternative.

- Hello Sarah, you're spoiling me, and with all these coffees I will not be able to sleep anymore.

- Saturday night at my house, there will be a party among friends, What would you say about joining us and taking away that gloomy expression from your face that you always take along with you? She asked.

- I don't know if I'll be free on Saturday, We have to conclude a major experiment with the team, we might be busy with it until Sunday; But if we finish before, I promise you that Saturday I will come to the party – not even he believed the words he had just spoken.

- I will be expecting you, and I'll make sure that your colleagues leave you free on Saturday.

They exchanged a kiss on the cheek and Alan went up the stairs leading out of the faculty.

Just outside the building the scented spring air welcomed him, the golden dome of the Basilica of the Sacred Heart reflected the rays of the sun at sunset, the effect was a kaleidoscopic color game that dazzled those who looked at it directly; golden light covered the roofs, and the outlines of the houses were blurred to the peripheral vision of the eyes; the trees slightly moved thanks to the light evening breeze with the leaves of the planar trees that moved and changed color.

The University of Notre Dame was founded by Father Edward Sorin, French priest of the Congregation of Holy Cross; it was a private Catholic university and was one of the most prestigious and important colleges in the United States. After having attended it Alan had become first Professor Ross's assistant, and later, when he retired, Doctor of applied physics. The main building dominated the campus with its Golden Madonna on the spire and the statue of Father Edward with open arms that seemed to want to protect his creature. Despite the spring, there were still piles of snow on the roofs and in the corners where the sun beat less, the building had been built in neo-gothic style with acute bow windows, everything was pervaded by a mystic atmosphere with the perennial cross present in every building. The multicolored stained glass windows of the Sacred Heart Basilica were made of mosaic and reflected the oblique light, creating on the cupolas angles illuminated with multiform colors that ranged from indigo to violet, from red to orange and dark corners, all the campus was immersed in the green and in the quiet. Alan walked to his BMW parked not far away and after have started the engine he headed towards home which was a few miles away from the university; traffic at that hour of the evening was intense, everyone was going back home after a day's work, but the lines of the cars were in order and the traffic flowed. Maybe the others had someone at home waiting for them, a wife, children, while he had no one, only his laboratory. Alan lived in a typical cottage of the area with the wooden boards of the facade painted white and the windows with green shutters, the house had three staggered constructions each with the roof higher than the previous one. The concrete road led to the garage, which was slightly off the main building, and was surrounded by a groomed lawn and decorative low-shaft trees. In the middle of the lawn stood, in its beauty, a large magnolia with its intense green leaves. Alan and Anna had bought the home together, or rather Anna's parents bought it, he could not have afforded it with the University's only salary. The garage led into the house and, through a staircase, to the subterranean floor that was larger than the overhead, a real bunker with concrete walls and small windows at the height of the ceiling that allowed the few rays of the sun, now dying, to enter.

With the remote control he activated the garage door and entered inside with the car, he rushed directly down the stairs to the underground room, a feeling of excitement pervaded him; This always happened when he had to wait for the result of an experiment. He went into the lab, a wild sound of *bips* welcomed him, a wall was full of monitors, and several computers were leaning on the workbenches, at the end of the long hall, you could see the controlled temperature room where the central server was located, directly connected via fiber optics and a firewall with the closest internet hub. This high-speed connection cost him several thousand dollars but it was vital for the operations that were done in the lab; In the right side of the room were placed various instruments, an electronic microscope and other equipment. In the center of the wall was an open door which led to another spacious room where was a micro-accelerator of low-energy particles that formed a ring underneath the house and which was used to test the behavior of any sub-atomic particles by emitting ion bundles; Nothing comparable to the Geneva CERN accelerator or the Stanford Linear Collider, but it still did his honest work. The environment was completed by a bathroom, a kitchen with a table and a sitting area with a sofa and armchairs.

The lab with all the equipment was a joint expense for all colleagues, much of which was covered by Gustavo Ortiz, of rich family, who had contributed decisively to the acquisition of the machinery and the construction of the ring and the bunker. Alan approached the computer monitor to look at the results and remained interdicted. The experiment he was conducting with his colleagues consisted in trying to prove that Schrödinger's quantum equation was false, or at least not completely true.

Quantum is the part of physics that studies the valid laws of elementary particles, in particular neutrons, protons, electrons and photons, according to this theory the behavior of the particles is in fact not precisely predictable but only in a probabilistic way, which instead does not happen with macro-systems made up of billions of particles.

Famous was the theory of the cat closed in a box under gunshot, that could be activated by the radiation of an uranium atom, you may not know when the atom will emit the radiation that will trigger the gun and kill the cat, in this way, the fate of the cat, which is a macroscopic system, will be ruled by probabilistic laws and therefore it can be said that the cat is simultaneously alive and dead at the same time; In a nutshell the five colleagues were trying to prove that this equation was not entirely true.

During their studies, though, they had changed their minds, they had noticed among the thousands of proven equations that there was one that meant not only that elementary particles were foreseeable but even controllable; In particular the equation seemed to pave the way to the levitation of objects by inhibiting the force of gravity.

They addressed their efforts in attempting to raise an object even a few millimeters by hitting it with rays, the computer had

10

to process the equation and then apply the result to the device that emitted them.

The whole trial environment was enclosed in an elongated glass bell in which vacuum was created to limit external interference, at the two ends of the bell were placed an anode and a cathode that emitted the rays that struck the object, this was represented by a lightweight titanium strip placed in the center of the bell, the titanium being ideal because it is a light metal with a white color, corrosion resistant, with a relatively high melting point. The computer usually took about three hours to process the equation, and if everything worked, the titanium strip would rise slightly from the plane, a sensor placed under the titanium plate would have indicated that there was a shift. Alan examined the metal strip, which was completely on the right of the glass bell; checked the computer's results, the sensor indicated that the strip was leaning on the bottom and had not stood up, it had not worked and apparently he had inadvertently moved the strip, yet he had been careful and was sure that when he left the strip was positioned exactly in the center of the bell: something was not right, but what?

He raised the glass case and repositioned the strip at the exact center, closed the bell and recreated the vacuum, went to the computer, and gave the ignition control of the rays with the same parameters used before, after a short squeeze of the electrodes, the strip returned to its original position on the right. Astonished, Alan repeated the procedure three more times, getting the same result every time.

Then he decided to put the titanium strip to the left of the glass bell, pressed "Enter" on the keyboard, and the strip moved immediately to the right; His eye had not perceived the movement.

He scratched his thoughtful beard, left the strip on the right, changed a parameter, and sent it to the computer; the strip moved instantly to the left.

So the movement could be bi-directional; He decided to make a further test; He opened the glass bell and moved the electrodes to a distance of five meters from each other, repeating the whole procedure.

The strip moved from one side to the other.

How it worked was clear, less clear was the reason for this behavior; He decided to change the material, took a metal nut, placed it and pressed enter ... nothing. He took a Lego block and repeated the procedure, with plastic it worked, he thought, could it be that the phenomenon was influenced by the mass? No, the block was much bigger than the titanium strip.

It could have been the kind of material, but he immediately discarded this hypothesis, plastic and titanium had nothing in common; Maybe the weight? It could be, but it would take months to find a solution.

Chapter 2

Martin Martino, an IT and telecommunications professor, that evening had to go get his daughter Laura who had dined at a friend's house, got in the car and turned on the engine of his old Ford. Martin was a genius in his field and, like all geniuses, he had aspects that opposed with his state, he was always distracted and his head in the clouds, sloppy when it came to fashion and personal care. He had enormous shoulders, thin hair, of indefinable red, always disheveled, his face full of freckles he looked like someone who drank too much, but Martin was a nondrinker and he never touched a drop of alcohol in his life. He might even seem a little autistic if you did not know him well, he always had algorithms in his head and always something to solve, he could think of multiple problems simultaneously and solve them simultaneously. Friends called him Bear, both for his appearance and for his exaggerated strength.

He walked into the driveway to enter the main street, his standard run was 25 miles per hour in the city and 40 out of town, he would hardly have get a fine for speed.

He had walked a few feet when the phone rang: "Hello Martin, it's Alan, do you have two minutes for me? - He perceived a note of euphoria in his friend's voice; Martin had been very close to Alan when Anna died, he had spent whole nights at his house, had even slept there trying to cheere him up , he knew he would not get great results but could not leave him alone, he was his best friend . They had attended university together and together they had shared beautiful moments and bad moments, they were very in tune and they did not need many words to understand what the other thought.

- Hi Alan tell me, I'm in the car I'm going to pick up Laura.

- You know that equation I told you about that flickered in my head and that I could not grasp? Well, I finally got it and I applied it.

- And ...

- And I think we made an unimaginable discovery.

- Don't keep me hanging, what happened?

- The strip has shifted from side to side of the bell, perhaps quantum entanglement is not just a theory.

- Interesting!

- Let me explain - Alan said, and explained to his friend what had happened to the titanium strip.

- Do you mind warning the others of the team? I'll call Freddy and I'll call Professor Ross, if he wants to come down, we could use his expertise, I don't think he will resist once I inform him. And don't forget the appointment for Wednesday, it becomes important now, I have to go down and try to figure out how it works.

- Sure I'll call them, fuck Alan ... I can't wait!

When he finished all the phone calls, Martin had driven over 40 miles his daughter's friend's house.

13

Chapter 3

John Davis walked down the stairs which from the upper floor led to the lower floor of the house where he lived with his wife and two male children, went to the bar and poured a generous dose of Jack Daniel's, he usually drank it with ice but that night he poured it pure. Things were not going well and he was worried, the news he had received that morning from General Clifford was very bad, indeed the worst he could receive, the congressional commission gave him three months to present the working prototype of the new shuttle engine, in case he did not succeed the federal funds would be cut off and he would find himself in a disaster. Rather he was already under the gun, he was struggling to pay the employees and his wife continued to squander money in beauty care, jewelry and expensive clothes, he wanted to tell her that he could no longer afford this life , but he could not find the courage; moreover, both children at college were an unsustainable cost.

He had tried to ask for funds to his father-in-law, Senator Andrew, but had received a mock laugh in response, Indeed his father-in-law had rubbed it in, bruising his plebeian origin and the inability to let his daughter and grandchildren lead the life they were accustomed to; So he had to hear him call him an inept and an incapable. John had never liked the Senator, he was aware of it, but the situation required him to throw away his self-respect to try to enter the graces of his father-in-law, but the results were not brilliant.

The corporation was called "Future Tech Inc." and he was the CEO and founder, the corporation's lab was struggling to find a solution for that damn engine, once it consumed too much, once it had a little boost, once it broke down as soon as it was turned on. For months the best designers and the best motorists had been working on the government's deal and still did not see the any chance of success, John had taken the best minds that cost him an arm and a leg, yet the results were zero.

He had created a company from scratch that had a turnover of several million dollars, working mainly on the engines of automobiles and carrying out a slow corruption of public officials and business executives, oiling congress and committees, and everything had always worked out perfectly. Then that damned order came and John had to satisfy his ego by accepting it, even though he knew he did not to have a structure suitable for that kind of project, but if he had succeeded, he would have become a thousand times richer than he was now and above all, it would have been right in the narrow circle of men that counted. But his dream seemed to start to fail with all the consequences that would have come, he had to find a solution but he did not know where to begin, the next morning he would go to the office and give an ultimatum to the engineers.

Chapter 4

Mary Russell received Martin's phone call while she was getting ready to go out; she usually paid much attention to how she looked, that evening she was paying particular attention, in fact she was expecting Jeff, a boy she had met in a bar.

Jeff was the classic American guy: wide shoulders, taurine neck, blond with blue eyes, emanated strength in every movement. He had approached her in the bar, asking her if he could buy her a drink, Mary scrutinized him from head to toe and decided that it would be worthwhile to take a ride with him. They had three drinks, chatted, then Mary had invited him to her home without hesitation, they had made love; Jeff had proved to be good as he promised, and Mary had decided that he would be a good companion for a couple of days.

She did not like this aspect of her personality, but she could not avoid it, she knew that she would regret it the next morning, but it was always like this and there was nothing she could do.

Since high school Mary had always been curvy, tall, a blond girl with explosive breasts, she attracted men like flies around honey, and she frowned on all those groomers who urged her vanity.

But she also had a brain out of the ordinary, she did not fit the saying "beautiful but stupid," she was intelligent and very brilliant, graduated in quantum physics at Stanford University with the highest grade, she soon went to work at Federal institute for pure research.

Her biggest torment and pleasure were men, she thought she was superior to most of them in terms of intelligence and she used them to her liking, but then when she deepened the relationship then she became fragile and completely at the mercy of the man, But she got tired soon and she would go back to being alone until the next conquest.

With Jeff, however, it was different, she had not yet gotten tired of him, that man had something different, magnetic and with a deep wickedness in the eyes, this mix of beauty and badness made her crazy, not that he had ever been bad with her but she imagined him so.

- Hello Bear, what's up?

Martin explained to her the result of Alan's experiment and reminded her of the appointment for next Wednesday.

As soon as she put down the phone, Mary's mind got to work at maximum speed and she completely forgot about the date with Jeff.

***

Gustavo Ortiz moved the pawn forward of a square on the chessboard that he had on the table, from the overview from above he realized that his opponent was losing the match, satisfied he repeated the move on the computer screen where it would be sent to the screen of his challenger, thousands of miles away. He had been playing for months with a Russian who really good at chess, their matches lasted for an infinity, Gustavo did not have much time, but as soon as he could he sat at the computer and made one or two moves. When he was playing, he did not like being disturbed and always turned off the phone, only to turn it back on as soon as he realized that his opponent was not online and that he would have to wait for his next move before continuing the game, so then he turned on the phone and turned off the computer .

And so he did that night, as soon as he turned it on, the phone sent two signals, one was a telephone company's phone message that warned him there was a call, the other a message from Martin's Whatsapp; He tried to call his friend but the line was busy, he would call him back later.

***

Fred Perry was named like the famous tennis player but they had nothing in common with him, he was rather lazy and habitual, he lived in South Bend just like Alan and was a physics teacher like him, he was a bachelor and his only company was a Two-year-old German Shepherd named Wolf. Fred was bald and had a bit of belly, tendentiously indolent, he loved to eat, taught at the University of Notre Dame.

He was walking the dog when the phone rang.

***

Gina Wood, a math teacher at the University of Illinois in Chicago, was busy in her Burraco nigh game with her friends when her phone rang, it was Martin. Gina apologized to her friends and stood up from the table to answer.

Chapter 5

Alan Adams spent all night in the lab drinking a mug of coffee, smoking four cigars and half a bottle of scotch, but he was still missing something. If he repeated the experiment with the set parameters, the titanium strip moved, but if he changed just one of the parameters, the phenomenon did not reproduce, yet it should have worked the same, why did that not happen? The parameter that had to change from time to time was not very meaningful to him, and it did not appear consistent with the rest, but if he changed it, nothing worked, Alan did not understand why changing something insignificant would affect the rest of the process. The next morning he did not have lessons and decided to stop because he was no longer lucid, so he went to the kitchen and prepared an abundant breakfast with eggs, coffee and orange juice, then sat on the couch and fell asleep.

TUESDAY

Alan woke up late that morning with a terrible headache: "I pay the excesses of last night " he thought; He took a shower and changed his clothes, took another coffee and felt much better. He was undecided whether to go back to the lab or to take a walk in the open air to clear his mind, the temptation to go down was strong, but he preferred the last option, it seemed to him the most appropriate solution; He grabbed his jacket and went out into the clear morning.

***

John Davis came into the office with a grim air, his collaborators already knew his mood swings and they simply greeted him "good morning." He went into his office without greeting anyone, after a moment his secretary Priscilla walked inside with his cup of double coffee- Seeing his mood she did not even try to remind him of the day's appointments, she put the drink on the table and left the room .

After only five minutes John called her and she rushed.

- Priscilla call all the engineers and tell them to be in the meeting room in an hour please.

- Certainly Mr. Davis, in an hour in the meeting room, I shall reming you that at 10 o'clock you have an appointment with the

Power Engines CEO for that hypothesis of merger ," Priscilla said with a professional tone..

- Cancel all appointments of the day.

- But this appointment has been scheduled for months, if we cancel it now it will take months to get a new one.

- Do as I told you – said John, abruptly.

Priscilla left the room, he took the phone and dialed a number he knew by heart.

- Hello... It's Davis, I'll need your services soon, make yourself available.

He put the phone on the handset and it rang, only a few people knew his direct number, so he answered without delay.

- Davis, who am I talking to ? - He said, listening.

**

Mary woke up and stretched like a cat, her body fluttered as she stretched out the muscles, she felt good after the night spent with Jeff, it had been a long night and she had slept really little, they had talked for a long time and Jeff had turned out to be smarter than she thought. Mary had told him of her work and he had been very interested, asking her proper questions that showed sufficient knowledge of the matter, however he never talked about himself. Jeff had already left, so Mary got up, took a shower, had a cup of tea, and thought back to what Martin had told her.

Chapter 6

Alan walked toward the park, the air was warm, and the buzzing of the bees that had to catch the acacia trees in bloom could be heard all over, the insects lay on a flower, took a few moments, and then flew away towards another flower. Tireless, they would have tinned until the pollen collected had been too difficult to carry, then they would fly off not to another flower but to the hive, where they would deposit the booty that the bees would take care of, a perfect collaborative society in which democracy did not exist nor the social ladder, if you were born a worker you would die a worker, it was almost like what was happening in the globalized society. With these thoughts in mind he sat down on a bench and lit a Tuscan cigar, the acacias sent an intense smell that came to his nostrils, mixed with the smell of cigar tobacco, it was a mix of a blast; all around the white flowers blown by the rays of the sun glowed at the eyes.

After he smoked it all, he turned it off with the tool and he put it back in his mouth, he went to a bar to take another coffee, he would return to the lab soon to continue the work, he headed for the bar and went in.

Inside, the room was very soft and quiet, he ordered his coffee and after drinking it he decided that it was not time to return to the lab, it was like cultivating the expectation for an event, he wanted to extend the pleasure of waiting. He left the room and headed for Bend Avenue towards the best Italian restaurant in South Bend, Parisi's, he wanted a carbonara and then he would go back to the lab. He headed for the restaurant that was twenty minutes away by foot from where he was, when his cell phone rang, it was Sara.

- Hello Alan, where are you? Can we have lunch together?

Alan had no desire to eat lunch with her, but he thought could not mortify her again, she was caring and worried about him, while he was unfriendly to the limit of rudeness.

- Sure, Sara, gladly, I'm going to Parisi's, if you want meet me there

Sara accepted with enthusiasm and said that it would take half an hour to get there

After twenty minutes Alan had reached to the restaurant, but Sara was not there yet so he sat on a bench; After ten minutes, as promised, she arrived with her small Mazda, they exchanged a hug and a kiss on the cheek and entered.

Parisi's was a low rise building in the classic South Bend style, it was an Italian restaurant but decorated in Irish style, the environment was warm with wooden panels and paintings on the walls, the dishes were not exactly as Alan remembered them in Italy but they were passable and tasty. They sat at a table and ordered *bruschette* and carbonara and a bottle of Chianti Antinori.

The lunch went by pleasant and Alan forgot about the lab and the experiment, the conversation was pleasant and relaxing, they finished their lunch and they went for a walk arm under arms chatting, time went by in a flash and evening came, it had been a long time since he felt so peaceful and relaxed, he was fine with her and slowly lowered his defenses. He found himself walking toward Sara's car to spend the night with her, he could not imagine that would be the last day of calmness.

Chapter 7

That evening, Fred left the house to walk the dog, he walked past the driveway which led to the park, Wolf, happy for the walk, marked all the trees, then would run forward, stop suddenly to make sure that the master was following him, reassured he resumed the race towards the next tree. He had the strange feeling of being observed, he looked around but, apart from some health fanatic who was jogging and who was not looking at him, he was alone.. The park was not much illumined by the sparse streetlights that had a yellowish light, the fog was rising, and the contours began to blur. The city was quiet enough and he did not remember episodes of aggression but you could never know if some drug addicts or habitual delinquent wanted to rob him out of nowhere, he was helpless ... apart from the dog.

He did not have a great body and his laziness had come to make his body flabby and unattractive, even during college, while other companions played basketball or baseball, he preferred books and some good burgers. He heard steps behind him, they made a sound against the driveway gravel, they did not seem to accelerate but there was someone behind him.

"Don't worry, it's probably someone jogging," he thought, without being too convinced, he hurried to reach the nearest street lamp and called the dog; Wolf did not answer and he called him again.

- Wolf, Wolf come here boy, come on.

But the dog did not arrive, maybe he was running after some animal, Fred was getting worried and even scared, maybe it was the suggestion.

He reached the lamppost and looked around ... no one, but the fog made the visibility poor, he could not see more than ten feet away, he heard the steps again making noise on the gravel, then he heard other steps come from the other side, A bird flew away emitting a raunchy cry. An insect stung him on his neck, He chased it away with his hand, but he never got to carry out the movement because Fred blacked out suddenly.

Chapter 8

Nathan Smith smoked nervously inside the car with the lowered window, at his side Erwin Johnson snorted in a subtle way, it was already 2am and the fog made the vision difficult; from where they were they saw the entrance of the house, but until that moment they had not seen anyone, they had been waiting since 4 pm for someone to show up.. By now Nathan felt an impelling the need to empty the bladder, he got out of the car, taking care to turn off the interior light switch, headed to the tree under which the car was parked, approached the trunk, unbuttoned the flap, and peed with a grunt of satisfaction. He closed the flap, stretched his arms up and he got inside the car, looked at the phone to see the messages, all the teams had finished the job except one, he would have waited for daytime to return to the base.

WEDNESDAY

Alan woke up, he felt comfortable, Sara lay beside him, all curled and still deeply asleep.

He got up and went to the kitchen to make breakfast, made a strong coffee, toasted bread with butter and jam, orange juice, then with a tray he took breakfast in the bedroom.

–   "Good morning," Sara said sleepily
–   Good morning, have you rested well?
–   I slept like a hump, - she replied, looking at the clock. - My God, it's too late! This morning I had lesson at first period - she jumped out of bed and slipped into the shower.

He had a lesson that morning too, but it started at ten and he took it easy. Sara left running, saluting him with a kiss, he stayed a little longer, then went down the stairs, got out and lit a Tuscan. He picked up the phone from his pocket and dialed Martin's number.

"The customer you called is temporarily unavailable, please try again later," answered the recorded voice.

"Maybe he's in a place where there's no signal," Alan thought; While walking he tried to dial Ortiz's number, the same result, even in this case the client turned out to be unavailable. Then he called Mary but got the usual automatic answer.

"They all decided not to be found" He kept walking towards home and no longer thought about it, he had to go to school and the experiment would have to wait.

He walked into the park, heard the birds sing, spring was awakening, and the birds were coming to the egg-hatching time,

23

all of them waving as they fluttered from one tree to the next. The park was lonely at that hour, the roads that crossed it were deserted, the tall trees had already laid the leaves.

To get home Alan had to cross the park, a forest and then the St. Joseph River; He walked into the thickest woods, he lived on the left side of the water course and had to cross the pedestrian bridge joining the two banks.

He was in sight of the deck when he heard footsteps behind him, another man was making his way, but the hair on his back rose up, that was a feeling he always had in alert situations when there was something wrong. He had learned when he was under the Marines to be careful of his instincts, so he set out with all the senses on full alert. He looked around and then turned sideways, the person behind him was still distant and around there he did not see anyone else. The bridge approached and he realized that if there had been a real danger, it would come from there, he did not understand why he felt so alarmed, but his sixth sense screamed for attention.

He was preparing to climb the first step of the bridge when the feeling grew, he turned and saw that the man had accelerated his pace and was much closer to him, as if he had made the last meters running; He also noticed that he was wearing an object to his mouth and in doing so he stopped. Alan knew immediately what it was, he got down just in time to avoid the dart that flew no more than thirty centimeters from his arm, the man was reloading the weapon. Alan looked around looking for something to defend himself with and at the same time he heard the quick footsteps of several men on the deck, they were still far away but they were quickly approaching. On the ground near the point where he had fallen, he found a branch, and underneath the branch a large stone that fit in one hand, a rounded round pebble, took them both, one per hand. The aggressor was about to fire another dart, so Alan protruded with the branch, but had to avoid the dart that would easily pass through the fronds, he could not hope to it would hit the branch.

As soon as he saw the launch he shifted to the side and started running towards the man, the dart missed him, he was about to touch the other man when he pulled an automatic pistol from under his jacket, it was a Glock 30s 45mm , He recognized it immediately, it was a deadly pistol: if the man could shoot, he would not miss him.

He dived forward with the branch and hit the man in the forehead before he could shoot, the other shouted but did not let the gun go, Alan still clasping the stone in his hand, hammered the arm holding the weapon. The man gave him a fist on the solar plexus that left him breathless, his opponent was standing up so he kicked him in the groin and in the chin, he squashed to the ground rolling his eyes in pain, Alan took the gun that fell not far away and for safety he kicked the opponent's head, then he escaped.

He turned and saw that at least three men were coming towards him, they were still far away. As he looked at the advancement of the three guys, he noticed that the man on the ground was getting up and pulling out another weapon, he pointed at him and fired, an acute pain shot up his left arm, he felt the blood flowing, He had hit him. He removed the safety lock from the gun, turned around, and put himself in the shooting position with both hands which held the butt of the weapon and legs apart, He fired in rapid succession, the four men threw themselves to the ground and he ran away, into the woods.

He had been running for a while, he felt that his breath was getting heavy, his wound was bad, but it helped to keep the adrenaline around. Occasionally he turned back, saw no one but he could not continue to run in like that, he had to catch his breath and try to stop the blood coming out. Alan looked around, he was out of breath, and yet it was not time to stop, he saw a majestic tree with a low branch and decided he would climb it. It was a risk, the enemies could find his position, but he had the gun and they had to be careful, he was a good shooter.

He climbed up on the tree until he was high enough, covered by branches and leaves but from where he could see the underlying ground. Alan put himself in a comfortable position, took out his Sardinian knife, Pattada, which he always carried with him and cut the inner liner of the jacket, obtained a wide strip, tied it around his arm to stop the bleeding and waited.

The senses on alert, the sweat that now covered his body, the drops falling down into his eyes, burning, even the birds had stopped singing; Around there was only silence.

He saw a man with curved stride advancing cautiously, he was on the right of his position, had a headset in his ear and heard him speak in a low voice, but could not understand what he was saying. The man looked around, looked at the bushes, and the idea that the fugitive was perched on a tree did not touch him, he advanced and talked. He was now next to the tree, Alan held his breath, aware that the other could have heard any minimum noise. He leaned against the tree and lit a cigarette; "By doing such a thing he must not be great professional," Alan thought, "but who are these men and above all what do they want from me, why did they try to catch me?"

No doubt they did not want him dead, otherwise they would shoot to hit and they would not use that crap that probably contained a narcotic, so they wanted to catch him alive. Already this was comforting but not calming, moreover how did they know where he was? He was a creature of habit, that was true, but that morning he had taken a different route ... of course! That was exactly what had saved him, most likely the group of men would have ambushed him at home, but since they did not see him arrive, they had explored the surroundings.

Two other men sprang from behind a thicket and walked towards the accomplice leaning against the tree, the fourth man, the one who had shot him, was no where to be seen. Alan could see them well, there was one who looked like the boss, he was very tall with wide shoulders, square jaw and massive head, Alan renamed it "Quadro". Another one was of low stature and and perfect hair that seemed to have just come out of the hairdresser's. the tallest came near the accomplice who was smoking and, without saying a word , he punched him, the man fell to the floor with a groan.

- Why did you lit the cigarette, you idiot! Shouted the one who looked like the boss. - Where did he go now?

The man on the ground got up and massaged his jaw. - Sorry, boss, but I did not think it was important, the doctor was no where to be seen, and I thought he was far away, running like a hare and I could not keep up with him.

- Of course, if you stopped smoking and did more exercise, you might be more fit, - said Quadro. - Have you looked around here? - He murmured.

–   Yes and there are no tracks, I also tried to be silent to hear the steps of him running but there is absolute silence, He has escaped by now.

–   Damn! it Now who's going to tell the boss that we've let him escape? - Said Quadro. The three of them headed in the direction they came from.

Alan had heard the whole conversation without moving a muscle, and now he was all indolent, but he did not dare to move. They could have pretended to go away to catch him unprepared as soon as he was seen, so he remained up on the tree for a long time until at some point, cautiously, without making any noise, he went down and silently walked to the opposite side.

He was all stiff, a short distance away there was a fountain with the statue of a Greek hero, and several birds where drinking from the pool that collected the water. He approached it, took off his jacket and shirt, the wound was shallow because the bullet had touched his arm without penetrating, he was losing blood but was a superficial wound, he washed and rested the patch tied up with the lining of his jacket, and he walked.

"And now," he wondered, "what am I going to do?", going home was not an option, Sara was at work, the only intelligent move was to go to the police.

He headed toward the Italian restaurant through the park, while walking he tried to dial again the phone numbers of his friends in sequence, but always got the same answer: "The customer you called is currently unavailable, please try again later", but How was it possible? "He wondered.

When he arrived at the edge of the park, instead of turning towards the restaurant, he decided to go to his bank to withdraw money while wondering what they wanted from him. He was not rich so a kidnapping for blackmailing purposes was to be excluded. Unless ... but of course, the news of his discovery had, somehow, leaked and those men were after that, that could be the reason. But why? It was an embryo project, it would take years of experimentation and study ... but yes!

Everything was clear now, and Alan understood the possible implications of his discovery which until that moment he had not considered. Once appropriately developed it would revolutionize the world of transport and the world in general, once set up, the goods would travel from one point to the other of the globe in a moment. The transport industry would have to be reset and not just that, if people could be moved, then airlines and car producers would be shut down. The oil industry, all Arab's money ... puf vanished into nothing. Now he understood why they were looking for him and why his friends did not answer their phone: they had taken them. But how did they know everything?

He approached the ATM, inserted the card and typed the amount and the PIN code. A note appeared on the display: "Sorry, but you have reached the maximum daily withdrawal limit," but he had not taken anything that day. Astonished, he walked inside the bank, took the number for the queue and waited for his turn.

When he arrived at the desk of the clerk, he looked at him, bored, from behind thick turtleneck goggles that highlighted wrinkles around his eyes.

    –   Can I help you? - He asked.

    –   I would like to make a withdrawal from my account.

    –   Your account number and an ID, please, - said the clerk. Alan told him the account number and pulled out from his pocket a driver's license, the clerk tapped on computer keys and rolling his eyes behind the lenses said - I'm sorry to inform you that your account has no funds, there was a withdrawal this morning of all your money, at this time the balance is zero - and returned the license to Alan.

    –   How is it possible? I did not make any withdrawals, can you see who did it?

The clerk, annoyed, looked at him again and, still pressing a few keys, said, "You took the money through your Home Banking, have a good day," he pressed the button for the next customer in line.

Alan knew he was in trouble, these people were very powerful, they had penetrated into his bank account and had drained it, he now had about only $ 200 in his pocket. He decided to call Sara but not from the cellphone, if these people were so powerful his cellphone could be traced. He left the bank looking for a public phone, insert the quarter coin and dialed the number, the phone inevitably reported the usual voice to tell him that the customer was unavailable. Had they taken for her too? No, simply she was in class and had turned off the phone, he had to go to Sara, to reach her at the university.

He looked around for a cab, but a doubt overcame him immediately, if they were looking for him then there could somebody on guard at the university waiting for him, it was also true that the university was very large, had two lakes and about 143 buildings, But Sara taught in the same building where he taught and they would have waited for him there.

There was no way to get around the obstacle, the entrance was one, in his memory there were no other entrances, so he could not go there; The only solution was to wait for Sara to finish the lesson and to go home, from where he would call the police.

He called a cab and gave Sara's home address, but he got off a block away. The houses were all the same or very similar, which meant a great lack of imagination by the designers, they were pretty but monotonous. Hiding himself in the shade of a tree, Alan looked around trying to see some suspicious car parked or some nearby people, but he did not see anyone, after all his neck did not pinch.

The woman lived in Granger, just off South Bend, almost on the edge of Michigan in a typical cottage similar to Alan's. The house had a tilt with two protruding sides, triangular, in front of the entrance door there were two columns that supported it, in a classic American style. It was a two-story house and had dark edges, there were also two small cypresses at the sides of the door, at the foot of one of these cypresses there was a stone under the key, Alan took it and went in.

He went to the fridge and drank a sip of water, then decided to have a coffee. When he put it on the stove he thought that perhaps Professor Ross would have advised him for the best. Could he take the risk of informing him? Maybe yes. Ross lived in California, he called him and told him about the experiment. It was unlikely that anyone who was following him could link him to him, the same could not be said for Sara; Alan tried to check as soon as he heard the car arrive, there were still least two hours to go before her return.

He picked up the house phone, he did not trust his cell phone anymore and had turned it off. He dialed the number of

Professor Ross. In California it was 8.30 in the morning, but Ross was no doubt awake.

After a few rings, the professor's voice answered.

– Professor, It's Alan and I'm in trouble, - he began.

– What's going on, Alan, are you okay?

– Certainly Professor, I'm fine, but now please listen to me without interrupting it. I have to make you aware of a matter that is endangering my life and that of my friends.

He told him the whole story of the ambush he had suffered, of his friends who did not answer the telephone and his suspicions.

After listening carefully Ross said, "Who is aware of this?"

– Only the colleagues with whom I do the experiment,- said Alan.

– And you are sure that no one of them told it to someone?

– Oh God no, I can't rule this out but it seems difficult that one of my colleagues went to report a news that is still to be proven right.

– Yet someone must have known about it and has seen before you did the potentialities thus deciding to take possession of it. Of course he can't do it without you and without your friends, so they tried to kidnap you. With you they have not succeeded but if you tell me that the others are not reachable on the phone, maybe with them they have succeeded, you have to make the news known. I would make a phone call at the South Bend Tribune telling what happened, but I would not go to the police.

Alan thought of what Ross had said to him, and after a brief silence he said, - But you realize that they have managed to clear my bank accounts in a flash, do you really think that they have infiltrated the police too? And what about the newspaper, You think they'd believe me if I started out with "Hi, I'm Dr. Alan Adams and I made an amazing discovery," I don't think this is a good idea. I thought instead of going to the police And then you

31

should announce it, it would be all different, they would believe you. I have all the parameters of the experiment in the USB key and I would like to ship it to you by mail, at this point I don't even trust e-mail.

- Maybe you're right, but to send me the results to spread them does not make you safe from those people, you have to find a safe place to stay and never go out until you're safe or until you find out who these people are. I have a friend at the FBI, I will try to talk to him, no doubt he is more experienced than we are in these things; Meanwhile buy a pre-paid mobile phone and then give me the number, break yours, is not enough to keep it off, then come to me.

Chapter 9

Ross had retired to a small California town named Woodlake, the place was called so because it stood near a pond, Bravo Lake, which was a little bigger than a puddle. The town was located in San Joaquin Valley, in the Tulare County, the lake was mostly used for the irrigation of fields, being the arid climate and the crops in need of water. In his valley with olive trees and vineyards, he helped make the village bucolic, when Ross had retired, he had bought a farm just a few feet from the water and the other side of the village; The house was rather isolated from the others and surrounded by cultivated fields, the country's homes were similar to those of South Bend but much more humble and less cured.

Ross lived in that place for five years. His wife had died four years earlier, his only son working and living in New York. They would see each other once a year. He did not miss his son so much but rather his grandchildren. Sometimes he wanted to take the plane and go see them, but then the fear of causing trouble To his son and daughter-in-law kept him from going. The daughter-in-law specially seemed annoyed whenever she saw him and he did not go willingly at their house.

He spent his days studying and fishing at the lake, he was a minute man with lively black eyes and white, smooth hair, now shaved, he was a person who at first sight breathed calm and security, had not integrated much in the life of the town, But loved the tranquility of that place and he was fine there.

Chapter 10

Jo Laganà was an Italian native by now of third generation, he lived in Chicago where he had his headquarters, he was a professional criminal with multiple ramifications in various disciplines, from trafficking to prostitution from gambling house to killing for hire. He was affiliated to the Racconiti family one of the oldest associations of the 'ndrangheta in the US. and that day he was coordinating the operations his acolytes were doing or were about to accomplish.

The news they received was mostly good, but the doctor had escaped the kidnapping and that incompetent of Rocco had made a chaos, as always moreover, professor Gina Wood was in fact dead after she was narcotized. Jo did not know if his men had used an excessive dose of narcotic or if Wood had had an anaphylactic shock, being possibly allergic to some substance, yet she was dead; His men had made the body disappear, buried in a forest.

This did not affect the order, but if they could not capture the doctor it would all have been useless and Davis would not pay. But the doctor had little chances, they were able to drain his bank accounts, his friends were taken, he was alone and without money and would soon fall into their net. Jo left the office and started walking toward the usual restaurant where he usually dined. He had a stout body with a prominent belly, he did not speak Italian, but had kept the Italian habits of his region, only he had taken the

33

worst of the two worlds. Someone sent to him the nduja and the chili from Calabria, then put it on the burgers and in the pasta he put ketchup. He put the chili on the steak and added the mustard to the carbonara. At the usual restaurant they knew him well and prepared for those brews that he liked so much, everyone wondered how he could eat that stuff.

Chapter 11

Martin woke up with a mouthful taste of burnt rubber, he tried to open his eyes but they were glued. He had his throat ripe and he wished ardently to drink something. He did not understand where he was, the air was damp and cold. When he finally opened his eyes, he realized he was lying on a bed, over a messy and broken mattress, a naked lamp hung from the ceiling hanging on a thread, the light emanating was dim and barely allowed to see in the room, a spherical camera placed in a corner attached to the ceiling had the red led turned on and turned off. He looked around, the room was large and there were five more beds, three lined up in the wall in front of him and one next to his, empty.

The other beds were occupied by two men and one woman but he could not see who they were. They were sleeping deeply.

He tried to emit a lure, but nothing came out of his throat, the other bodies began to move, the room had an iron door, and a small window on the top, he tried to get up but couldn't and he abandoned himself again on the bed.

Chapter 12

Alan stood by the window awaiting Sara's arrival, meanwhile he rummaged about the possible solutions, His analytical mind examined all the options and discarded them one after the other, the only salvation was represented by her, that is if they had not yet connected her to him. Then yes, his situation would get more complicated.

He had no money, and the escape to reach Professor Ross had to be done via car, he even thought of somewhere isolated where to hide momentarily, but he did not think of anything.

He turned on the television to the news channel.

"… the body of a man with a deep wound to his head caused by a blunt object, most likely a stone next to the corpse, was found in the park this morning. The object is now in the hands of the investigators, fingerprints are being searched for. The man had no ID on him and for the moment it has not been possible to proceed to his recognition, according to some witnesses a man has been seen fleeing the scene of the crime, who is currently being looked for. According to an identikit carried out by police experts, the assassin could correspond to a man about a meter and eighty-five, medium-sized and with dark hair or dark brown and a beard, dressed in a gray jacket and jeans; – The identikit appeared on TV: it was him.

But he did not kill that man, the TV reporter continued: "The man is armed and dangerous, all those who have information are asked to call the number …"

They had framed him, now the police were looking for him. He examined the Glock, checking how many bullets were left in the loader, only a few. He needed more and he had to try to disguise himself somehow, whoever was looking for him had important connections in the FBI, he had to wait for Sara.

It was just past 1 PM when he heard the noise of the little Mazda, he opened a shutter and peered out. Sara got out of the car, he checked outside looking around the street but he did not see anyone, For precaution he did not look away from the window not even after she got home.

– Hello, what are you doing here? My God … you're hurt!

35

He took her hands, sat her down and began to explain. "Now, listen to me carefully, Sara, because what I am about to tell you has endangered my safety and yours.

He told her everything. She did not ask any questions, then he asked her to go out and run the necessary errands

- You have to go to the post office and make an urgent package to send to Professor Ross, you have to buy some clothes for me and a light brown hair dye, then you have to go to the munitions store and you have to buy a box of these bullets, go to the bank and collect all the cash you can and then put gas in the car, also buy some bandages, disinfectant, antibiotics and a razor..

She looked at him apparently without understanding. - Let me see this wound, - she said apprehensively.

- It's just a scratch, don't worry, I just need to put a bandage on it and put it an antibiotic ointment.

Sara left the house to run the errand he had asked for. Left alone, Alan thought of the whole story, someone had talked about the experiment, but he could not imagine who might have been, none of his friends were very inclined to reveal secrets, they were all trusted and he knew them for years, but some had been doing too much talking, perhaps inadvertently .

He sat down, the adrenaline had almost disappeared from his body and he began to feel tired and restless, thinking about all the events of the last few hours and how it all happened so quickly.

He heard Sara return with the purchases, he took the clean clothes that she had brought him and went to the shower.

– Did you find everything? - He asked.

– Yes, except that I could not take all the cash, but I got enough, I will let the university know that I don't feel very well and I will take a few days off

– Why? He asked, perplexed.

– I'm coming with you

– Not a chance! You'll be more useful to me if I know you're safe.

– Alan, I'm coming with you, you will not be able to get rid of me.

The man with a shoulder-strap headed toward the bathroom. After showering and shaving he colored his hair, he medicated, he dressed and together they left the house, heading toward the car, He sat at the driver's seat and started slowly toward their destination. Alan scrutinized the surroundings but saw nothing suspicious, set the route on the navigator, took the main avenue that would take them a few miles off the freeway.

As soon as they left, a car broke away from the sidewalk where it was parked and started in the same direction.

Chapter 13

Mary Russell woke up, she could not open her eyes, she still felt that same torpor that takes you over in the morning when you slept so deep for eight hours, she felt confused and her mouth tasted of medicine, she did not remember what had happened. She remembered that she had left home and then nothing more, the void. She tried to gather her ideas, she spent the night with Jeff, this she remembered, but then?

She managed to open her eyes, she was on a bed in a bare room, the concrete walls were filled with damp spots and there was a lamp hanging on a thread that illuminated the environment, the mold of tan filled the air. She turned to one side and opened her eyes, she saw five beds with four of her friends, Ortiz and Fred were sleeping while Martin was awake and he stared at her.

- Hello Mary how do you feel? He asked in a kinky voice.

– Martin I don't remember anything, I just know I have a big headache.

－ We are trapped, prisoners I would say, I cannot reach the window and the door is locked, I tried to call but no one answered me, I don't understand why we are here, who kidnapped us and especially why.

- It is useless to get agitated, sooner or later someone will show up, I'm also a bit hungry, - Mary said.

Meanwhile, Fred was awakening, emitting grunts as he tried to open his eyes, wriggled and emitted grunts, then managed to get out of his torpor, looked around lost and greeted his companions.

- Don't tell me, they kidnapped us right? I remember that I was walking the dog in the park when I heard footsteps behind me, then someone struck me with something and I fainted, the dog did not answer ... if they did hurt him they will deal with me!

Soon after also Ortiz moved and woke up, and he too wondered what had happened.

- There's something weird about this story, we're all involved in the story of Alan's experiment. But he's missing and also Gina is missing. Perhaps they were not able to take them? Martin said.

- It seems to me that these people are very well organized, maybe they have not taken them yet, but I think it's just a matter of time" Gustavo replied.

- But if the reason for our kidnapping is to look into Alan's experiment, what do they hope to get from us? We don't know anything, it's all in his head, we don't know what he has done and what equation he has applied. And then it's just a sketch of an experiment we don't know how it works, we don't know what it is, practically we know nothing, "Martin said.

- Then, there is a question, how did they get the news, I did not talk to anyone, and you? – Gustavo said.

- Not me. Really, - Fred replied.

- Me neither ... - said Mary, Wait a moment. I talked to someone ... but it seems unlikely that Jeff understood in full what I told him. It's a pretty awkward guy, that's true, but he did not seem to understand the equations and the possible consequences, moreover I did not explain everything in detail.

- Who is Jeff? - Martin wanted to know.

- My last boyfriend, - Mary said, blushing.

The four researchers continued their conversation, not knowing that in a room not far away there was someone who did not miss a word of what they were saying and who was recording everything.

Chapter 13

Nathan Smith drank a sip of coffee and lit a cigarette, eagerly sucking a breath of smoke. The day had been intense and tiring, he looked at his helpless helper sleeping on the sofa and wondered how it was possible for a person to sleep at all times and anywhere in any position, he kicked him and Erwin woke up. - They woke up and are talking to each other, it's time to go talk to them, take the hoods - Nathan said.

Erwin got up and went to pick them up. Soon after, with the hoods on the head and guns in hand, they started towards the cell, As they walked through the corridor Nathan thought that this story had complicated much his situation. Now it would be all more difficult to carry it forward.

The four heard a key turn and shortly after the door opened, they saw two men with their hoods on their heads holding guns, one of them was much taller than the other, the shorter one held also a plastic bag and a tray.

- Good afternoon gentlemen, rise and shine, don't be afraid we have no intention of hurting you, we only need your cooperation, please forgive us if we had to use these not so orthodox methods to persuade you to follow us, but at the moment we had no alternative and not even the time to use more civilized methods. We brought you water and food, I think you might be thirsty and especially hungry, "said the tall man. The shorter man gave each one a bottle of water, then took the sandwiches he had in the tray and gave one to each of them.

- You know you won't succeed. This is kidnapping. we are very well known and sooner or later someone will notice our absence - threatened Ortiz.

– don't worry about this, it's our problem, We just want your collaboration, we can get it either with good or bad manners, your choice. If you cooperate we won't lay a finger on you.. Otherwise my friend knows a lot of ways to melt a tongue, right Robin?

- Of course Batman. I know my job well, leave them to me especially this beautiful lady and I assure you they will talk, - replied the shorter man with a lax laugh and a trailing accent that denoted his southern origin.

"Batman and Robin, if we were not in this situation, it would be almost comical" Martin thought.

- Now we'll leave you alone, we'll bring some coffee later and you'll tell us what we want to know," said Batman.

- I would like another sandwich, one is not enough for me and I'm starving- Freddy said.

- Robin, satisfy the black man. Heaven forbid that they complain of our hospitality, - said Batman.

While Robin appeared more effective and even less educated, Batman used terms that denoted a certain degree of education and of irony , but his voice was cold and sharp, He affected the friends much more than Robin's grim laughter, they realized that he was a cruel and determined man, and that he was in charge.

When the two guards left, the scientists ate and and drank in silence, looking at each other, The situation was clear but tangled. They all looked at Mary blaming her for what had happened without saying anything, but their looks were a mute accusation against the woman.

Chapter 14

Pat Blake was seated at his office desk and read a file about the homicide of some prostitutes from Georgetown, when Special Agent Kate Ball came in.

- Chief we have a thorny problem. They entrusted us with a case of murder, directly from the local police, I've already got pressures. It seems that an esteemed professor of Notre Dame is involved, so we are getting calls also from the university and soon there will be pressures from the political spheres, here is the file with all the information.

"It's a big fat pain in the ass". Pat thought. When the politicians were involved, they were a pain in the ass.. He set the file on the prostitutes' and took what Kate had left on the desk, opened it and began to read.

A certain Dr. Alan Adam had killed an unidentified man, there were witnesses who claimed to have seen a person escape from the crime scene corresponding to the doctor's description, his fingerprints had been found on the rock, he read everything and then called Kate.

Chapter 15

Davis was still in the office, waiting for a phone call and an important visit, He was alone, even Priscilla had left. He got up from his desk, headed toward the bar where a row of Scotch and American bourbon lined up, a bucket containing ice, took one of the glasses and put two ice cubes and decided for a Woodford Reserve, a precious bourbon of Kentucky. He poured out a generous dose and drank half in a single sip. The phone rang in that moment and he hurried to answer, raised the handset and listened. After the phone call ended, he continued to sipping the bourbon.

Shortly after, the door bell rang and he stood up to open, at the door there was Matt Burton's Private Investigator

- Good evening, Mr. Davis.
- Good evening Burton, follow me in my office.

They started toward Davis's office. - Please sit down, would you like a drink?

- Thank you, Mr. Davis, a single malt scotch please

Davis prepared the drink and brought it to the detective. He sat down and waited for the other to sip the whiskey. Burton picked up an envelope from the folder and put it on the desk without saying a word. Davis took the envelope, his hands trembling slightly, a veil of sweat bead his lips, He opened the envelope, in the first photo there was his wife Barbara who, kneeling and with her mouth open in a mute cry of pleasure, was making love with a man much younger than her. In the second picture they were seated at a bar table and he held her hand. In another they were holding hands and on the background you could see the motel where they where heading. He browsed all the photos and all were unambiguous.

- Who is the man?
- His name is Anthony Petricci and he works as a coiffeur at Roseland, he is twenty-eight years old.

It was the place where his wife went to get her hair done. He did not feel angry, he had loved his wife once, but he did not love her anymore, so it was not the jealousy that struck him but the lack of respect from her. He however had done worse, and continued to do so, he had a fix lover he maintained in an apartment of the Indian village and between the gifts and the rent of the apartment ti cost him a lot. In the past he had had many lovers, but that did not mean that his wife would not be punished for that offense, he would certainly punish her very and very hard. He paid the detective and greeted him, then turned off the office lights and headed home.

Chapter 16

After entering Jefferson Boulevard they arrived at Roseland where they took the I-80 highway, the trip would be about 3600 kilometers long and they would take turns driving. The evening air had cooled down and the warmth of the small Mazda kept a pleasant warmth inside the passenger compartment; The radio was tuned to the local All News channel, and at that moment the news was aired, after talking about international and national politics, the news went to local news.

"Still no news of the killer of the unknown man in the park, it seems from the identikit spread by the police he is Dr. Alan Adams, a physics professor at the University of Notre Dame. Dr. Adams is currently unavailable, anyone who has information on the fugitive is asked to report to the local police. The law enforcement authorities invite the doctor to turn himself in for clarification of his position and not to aggravate it. "

Sara and Alan looked into each other's eyes. - It was not me. I just hit him in the head and kicked him, but I did not hit him to kill him. It must have been his accomplices to stage the murder to make sure the police were looking for me too.

Sara did not say anything.

They had traveled a hundred kilometers, Alan looked at the mirror to see if they were being followed, but the cars were many and he could not tell if there was a car in particular putting them on their heels. After a few miles they entered Illinois. At least now they would be safe enough from the police. Soon they would enter the state of Iowa, then they would stop for the night.

They went on the highway when, near the Prairie City, they saw the sign of a motel. They decided to take the junction to reach it.

Prairie City was a small and insignificant city, with homes still in the style of South Bend. When they arrived at the motel they got out of the car and walked into the reception. Sara gave her ID and the clerk gave them the key to room number 23; She asked for information on where to dine, then they headed for their room.

The room was shabby with a double bed which had known better times, on the walls flourished a wallpaper with various types of fruit drawn on it, now it was yellow and ripped at various points. The bathroom was not in better condition: scrawny and messy. .

- Nice place, - Sara said.

After having refreshed and changed their clothes they went out to go to the restaurant indicated by the receptionist. They found it, they were unpretentious, entered and sat at a table from which they could keep an eye on the road. A rather old waitress approached them.

- What can I get you gentlemen? We have excellent steaks, scrambled eggs with bacon, sandwiches with a cream of peppers and bacon, burgers, apple pie, chocolate cake and coffee.

They both ordered a steak with a beer and a slice of apple pie and then plenty of coffee.

As they ate in silence, they saw the lights of a police car that was entering the parking lot. The two agents entered the restaurant, walked in and looked around, they pretended to talk to each other, in the restaurant only two more tables were busy. The agents approached the bar and ordered coffee and cake and started eating, sitting on the stools beside the counter. One of them carried the sheriff's star and looked around glancing at them, then approached their table with the cup of coffee in his hands.

- Good evening, I'm the Sheriff of the county, my name is Peter Zilosky, are you visiting for pleasure? He asked

- No, sheriff, we're passing, by we stopped at the motel that's down the road for the night, and in the morning we're hitting the roar, we're headed to California, - Alan said.

- A long trip via car, - he replied.

- My husband and I love traveling by car, this allows us to see places that we would never see via airplane, we can stop where we want and enjoy landscapes,- Sara added.

The Sheriff said, "Well, I wish you a good trip." He headed back to the counter, finished his coffee and went out with his colleague.

Once the two agents got in the car, the sheriff picked up the radio's microphone. "Station, Sheriff Zilosky speaking, can you check the license plate of a car? Thanks, I'll wait.

Sara looked at Alan. - Do you think he suspects something?

- I don't think the news of the murder has arrived here, I think we'd better leave the room right away and travel at night.

They paid and went to the motel, the air was cold despite the spring and their breath condensed into the smoke when they breathed, the motel sign blinked one letter at a time and then lit up all together, the "E" did not work. Each letter had a different color and when it got to the letter "M" that was of a bright yellow color or when it was all lit up, the light illuminated the square covered with gravel. They went in to take their suitcases.

Chapter 17

He was sitting in the driver's seat along with two men, the other car, with three other men, was not far ahead of them. The one sitting at his side had square shoulders, and even his head with that haircut recalled a cube, was a killer at the service of his father. They stood still, protected by a laurel hedge, but they

45

could see the motel square; They saw the Mazda arrive and stop at great speed and stood alert.

Rocco was Jo's son, he was good looking and loved the good life, his favorite pastime were women, betting on horses and frequenting night clubs. His father had bet a lot on him, his only male son, but he had always disappointed his expectations. Every task entrusted to him always ended up having some sort of bad outcome, he simply was not suited for the crime, even the relatively easy task of kidnapping Dr Gina Wood had turned out to be a disaster, the doctor was dead: but how was he supposed to know she was allergic to narcotic?

He had to prove to his father that he could be trusted, and this time he would not disappoint him, all he had to do was follow the doctor and the woman who was with him and kidnap them both at the right time and then deliver them alive, this was the only condition that had convinced his father to give him the job. In particular, the doctor was not to be harmed in any way. He wanted to hurry up because the new dancer he had meet at the club was waiting for him.

He saw the two leave the room with their suitcases and get on the Mazda in a hurry, so Rocco ordered at the first car to wait a few moments before going to the pursuit; As soon as the rear lights disappeared from the view the two cars set off. They had just taken the main road when in the rearview mirror Rocco spotted the police flashing at full speed entering the parking lot of the motel.

***

Alan had come out of the parking lot and had turned off the lights, shortly after he saw two cars entering the main road, then he accelerated as much as he he could without lights; Then instead of going straight he had taken a secondary road which according to the indication led to a picnic area in the woods.

Chapter 18

Pat Blake received the phone call from sheriff Peter Zilosky the moment he was about to go home, he had planned a long weekend with his wife and his son. He had promised him that he would bring him to the lake to fish. He had postponed fishing with him for weeks, his wife was very pissed. Unfortunately even this time he would have to postpone, he gently pulled off his overcoat which he had already slipped on and tried to call home. Meanwhile, thanks to the fingerprints they identified the man killed, he was a small criminal involved in a Chicago clan, the odd thing was that even the two witnesses were suspected, although there was no evidence that they belonged to the same clan. The matter was rotten, but first they had to track down the doctor. So Pat called Kate.

- We have to leave, gather the team - then he called home.

According to the sheriff's phone call, the car had been seen in a small Iowa country but the two had disappeared from the motel where they had taken accommodation, It seemed to be an escape, but who knows if it was an escape from the police or an escape from the clan. Pat suspected that the two were running away from the clan and not from the police, but the motive and the reason the two did not turn to the authorities remained a mystery . He was getting ready for a long night's work.

Chapter 19

The road was disconcerted and the car jumped on the roots of the pine trees on the sides that had invaded the roadway, rising to land on the ground until the next root. Alan looked in the mirrors and saw that the two cars had turned in the same street, he turned the lights on.

47

The pines ended and to the sides where the field was before, the woods began to materialize with spruce trees and imposing oaks, the two cars were gaining ground.

- Hold on tights Sara, Now we will dance a little.

Sara was curled up with her legs slightly raised and her hands clinging to the seat, she had a terrified expression on her face.

They passed a sign that invited them to turn right to reach the equipped picnic area, he drove straight, now the cars were no more than a hundred meters away but the Mazda could not run faster, There were no side streets, the woods ran with them like a green wall to the right and to the left. The cars got closer.

Suddenly the first car spurted them, making it jump, Alan tried to keep the direction turning the steering wheel, the car tried to flank them and he tried to move in the middle of the road to prevent the maneuver. The tire crashed at every curve, with a leap the chasing car almost flanked but Alan playing with the steering wheel managed to avoid it. " I can't go on like this for a long time," he thought, the car following them was a massive dark sedan, it looked like a Ford.

They went on like this for a time that seemed indefinite, suddenly the chasing car was able to side up with the Mazda that bounced off fearfully under the Sedan shots, the left wheels lost adherence to the ground and the car rose to the side. When it returned to the ground and the wheels were on the ground again, he suddenly drifted and pushed forward, at that moment began a series of curves and the road suddenly narrowed.   Another vehicle was coming from the other direction which honked furiously, It was a truck, the car that followed tried to move forward but Alan turned the steering wheel to cut it off; Meanwhile the truck came up with terrifying horns. By now the clash was close, at the last moment Alan turned the steering wheel to the right and he avoided the truck, the other car could not do the same and hit the other vehicle in a bumpy, bruised metal noise, then caught fire.

Alan tried to keep the little car on the road. He turned furiously the steering wheel but the car was no longer responding, the wheels where on the grass and ran without brakes parallel to the main road. It continued its race for a hundred meters then the ground beneath the wheels was gone and the Mazda fell into the river that ran softly minding its own business.

Chapter 20

Rocco avoided the clash, He nailed the car and got out of the way. The Ford had taken fire and for its occupants there was nothing left to do even if they had survived the impact.

- Mik, you take the car and turn it around, we must go back. It will be full of policemen here pretty soon. Dave come with me, let's see what happened to the doctor, if he is not dead we have to save him and capture him, and if he died we should leave, let's go!

The two men started running parallel to the road, ran to the bridge crossing the river and sprang out of the parapet. In the water they still saw the car's headlights on, the car was totally underwater now. Shortly after, the lights went out and the water swallowed up the Mazda, the river went back to its silence.

- Shit, shit, shit, shit, - cried Rocco with his tight fists and tightened jaws, "let's go back to the car and get out of here.

The two men started running, Mik was waiting for them in the car who in the meantime had turned the car on, they left with a squeak of tires.

Chapter 21

The car was sinking and Sara was screaming. Alan tried to open the windows first and then the doors but they were all locked. The water rose, Then he stood with his feet on the windshield and began to hit it ever stronger, leaned against the seat and hit, nothing happened, the windshield did not move, but he continued to strike. The water now came to his chest, he had to continue to beat the glass, He struck and then struck again, a small crack opened no bigger than a cobweb, he continued to kick it as the spiderweb widened. With a good shot, the windshield came out of the car, and Alan took Sara by one arm and slipped out.

The water was cold and muddy, they swam until the current dragged them under a bridge, Alan clung to the canes and stood in that stern position, to wait.

No noise was heard except the water's slippage, they broke away from the reeds and while well immersed they let the stream drag them.

Chapter 22

Nathan went into the prison room carrying a pot of coffee and paper cups, he asked whoever wanted it, everyone responded yes.

- Good! Now that we've finished socializing, let's talk about why you are here and what we need, we know that during your work with Dr. Adams you found the way to move objects, is it right?

Freddy was the first to answer: - We only know what Alan has told us, we don't know the procedure or the formulas he applied, we are useless for you and we can't help you in any way.

- Doctor let us decide this, if you have the formulas and parameters you can reproduce the phenomenon.

- Probably we could, but why should we do it, who are you, and why do you want us to reproduce the experiment? Said Mary.

- We belong to an international organization, of what kind You don't have to worry about, you have to do it to avoid unpleasant consequences. Soon you will be taken to a well-equipped laboratory and you will be provided with the data you need, when you have done the experiment, you will be freed and you will also be given an adequate reward. Keep in mind that at this moment your family members are kept under close observation and if you refuse to collaborate, they would also be involved. So do your evaluations well, we don't have time to waste, in an hour we will leave this place and take you to the lab, please don't resist.

Nathan left the room and walked outside the building, lit a cigarette, he had to devise a plan to resolve the situation without endangering the hostages.

Wednesday night

After being dragged by the stream, Sara and Alan found a place where the banks of the river moved away, the river creating a loop with a small pebble beach where the water was low. They approached, swimming to the bush and came out of the river, they were cold and now that the adrenaline was no longer circulating also very tired.

They looked around, the river had dropped them far down the valley, the woods were far and wide there were fields cultivated with corn. This was already tall and made the visual difficult. The moon was small up in the sky and It did not lit the environment, They did not know where to go, they took the road away from the river in the cornfields; If there was corn there would also be a farm, but no lights were nearby. After walking in silence for a while, the ground began to rise, continued in the same direction and came to a hill, here was a small oak forest, they sat down leaning against the tree trunk.

- What are we going to do now? Sara asked. - We have to look for help, there will be some nearby houses, we have to come up with an excuse.

Alan got up on an oak. On the other he could see a small light in the distance, the fog was raising , they decided to start in the direction of light.

They walked silently between the rows of corn, walked for a good half an hour holding hands, they came to a crop-less area. The light they had seen belonged to a farm, a tall building with the nearby dark red barn; The main house was a two-story, red as well. It filtered a dim light from one of the windows downstairs, a dog was barking furiously inside the house. The two fugitives came closer and the dog's barking became more furious, when they were about ten yards from the veranda, the front door opened. The dog came out, sniffing the air, but did not move.

- Stay where you are! shouted a woman's voice, who had appeared with a gun on the porch of the house. - Show yourselves, who are you?

- Good evening Madam, we had a car accident and ended up in the river, if you have a phone we would like to call for help, "said Alan.

- Come here, slowly, - she said, pointing the shotgun at them, then flipping a blinding light at them. They approached while the dog growled furiously.

- Good Buck, good.

When they arrived at the veranda the woman looked at them from head to toe like an investigator.

- We don't want to disturb you, we only need you phone and then we'll leave. don't be afraid, lady we have no bad intentions, "Sara said.

- And where do you want to go looking like that? Come inside and get warm. You look pretty battered, I recognize the

52

good people from the eyes and you seem to me all but delinquents. Come on, I just put the teapot on the stove, I think a hot drink will please you.

They entered and the dog sniffed them, then obviously satisfied returned to his kennel near the fireplace and did not look at them anymore.

The house was simply furnished with antique furniture and some antique pieces that denoted an uncommon taste. Around the burning fire there was a couch and two worn-out leather armchairs, but they had to be very comfortable. A stairway led upstairs. Some paintings depicted hunting scenes with deer, elk and wild boar; The light was radiated by hanging lamps on the walls that were reproductions of old oil lamps. It was a warm and comfortable atmosphere.

- But do you live alone in this secluded place? Sara asked.

- Since my Peter went to heaven, I live alone and manage the farm along with my Buck, where do you want me to go after I've lived here all my life?

The woman was an old lady, she looked over eighty years old. Wearing a pair of round glasses resting on the tip of her nose, she had a fresh face for her age. Red cheeks denoted the healthy habits of an open-air life. A cascade of white hair twisted in natural curls.

- My name is Nora, - said the woman, stretching her hand to Alan - and you, young man, what's your name?

Alan presented himself and introduced Sarah, partly telling what had happened to him by sharing the story of a few truths and many lies. Finally he said, - And that's all that happened to us, a long day, so if you're so kind enough to let us use your phone, I have to make a few calls.

- Young man, now you do as I say, You don't seem in good condition, Drink your tea And then go upstairs in the first room to the right, there is a bathroom and two closets with clothes, take a hot shower, you need that. You can change if you find something that fits you, In the meantime I'll prepare dinner for you. Upstairs, go. there will be time To make a call.

Alan tried to protest but Nora, with authoritarianism, silenced him and pointed with her finger at the ramp of stairs leading upstairs.

Upstairs, at the end of the corridor, they found the room indicated by Nora, they looked at each other and despite the tension ,a smile appeared on their lips

- What a terrible old lady, authoritarian but also sweet, I would never have allowed two strangers in my house, - Sara said.

Then one by one they took a hot shower, found some clothes that fit well and went downstairs to dine.

Pumpkin soup smoking dishes with baking breads, wine, and a huge steak with fried potatoes were waiting for them. They began eating and they realized that they were hungry, very hungry. After they had finished the steak Nora brought them a piece of cake, Alan tried to refuse but she put a finger straight to her nose, gesturing to eat and be silent.

When the Lucullian dinner was over, Alan put his hands on his belly, he was full.

-- Young man do you smoke? Nora asked.

- Yes, madam, I smoke, but my cigars got wet in the river.

Then Nora, with a swirling step, headed toward the sideboard and returned with a box of precious Monte Cristo Cuban Cigars.

- My husband smoked them, may he rest in peace, I don't smoke, take one but go smoke outside, not even him I allowed to smoke in here.

"Poor Peter," Alan thought. But he took the cigar and went to the veranda, Sara followed him, sat in two wicker rocking chairs, he lit the cigar with satisfaction, shortly after Nora came up with two glasses of whiskey, followed by the dog.

The crickets sang in the silent countryside, no noise of cars or anything else. An owl tuned its song at regular intervals, it seemed that the air had stopped, there was no breath of wind and no leaf moved, they were in a suspended time, a bubble of tranquility and serenity but with a pending voltage charge.

- Such peace, - said Alan, - it reminds me of my in-laws' countryside, this silence, these smells are magnificent.

- I'm used to it. We usually don't appreciate what we have every day right under our nose, but I appreciate these places, actually I love them, I could not live in another place.

They remained silent, Alan smoked the cigar and drank his whiskey, and thought of everything that had happened. Sara caressed the dog who had become their friend.

- Now you two have a good night's sleep, in the morning you'll make the phone calls, then you'll take my van, it's old but it's still doing his job, it's not fast but it's strong, so with that you can reach California, I was going to change it.

- But no,- said Sara - you will be even more isolated, we will make it somehow, we can't accept.

- Girl, of course you can accept, if you take the van you'll get there earlier, but don't take the freeway, take the state road that is nearest. It will take you straight to California, now go to bed - and just like that,, followed by the dog, she went home.

Even Sara and Alan went to their room. They took their clothes off with some embarrassment, they lay in bed and fell asleep immediately.

THURSDAY

They woke up with a smell of coffee and fried bacon in the frying pan. They realized that despite dinner they were hungry, they went downstairs.

- Good morning! - Nora's voice welcomed them. - Have you slept well?

- Never slept so well,- Sara said.

- Breakfast is ready, I hope you like it ... there are eggs from my chicken, bacon and lots of coffee.

They ate with appetite, then Alan entered Peter's old office where the phone was, tried to call his friends first, but nobody was reachable, then he called Professor Ross.

They said farewell to their benefactress and started off with the snoozing and tramping van, it was rusty but the engine seemed to hold well, Nora and Buck saluted them from the veranda, they would never be seen again.

Chapter 23

The FBI Special Agent, Pat Blake, had reached Prairie City late in the morning, stopped with the other agents at a cafe for breakfast and to drink abundant coffee, they needed it after the sleepless night. Then, once they asked for directions, headed for the sheriff's office.

- Nice to meet you, I am Sheriff Peter Zilosky, - he welcomed him by stretching the hand to Pat,- we have news, the car was found in the river but there are no corpses on board, near the point where the Mazda fell into the river there was a scary accident, three charred corpses in a car and the truck driver is at the hospital, in reserved prognosis, he's in coma and at this time it is not possible to question him. From early evaluations it seems that the doctor's car has been involved in the accident and fell into the river.

- Well, let's go to the site.

Once they arrived on the spot, they found the Sheriff's men who had retrieved the car. Pat stepped off the road, approaching.

- The windscreen is broken, do you think it was the impact or was it broken to get out of the car? - He asked the sheriff.

- Apparently broken from the inside and not from the outside. So they either came out of there and they have gone away or the current has dragged down the corpses, my men have searched a good stretch of river, but the two have disappeared.

Having returned to the village and taking accommodation in the only hotel there, they went to the sheriff's office.

- I have organized search teams who are looking around the neighborhood, if they find something, they will warn us - said the sheriff. All that was left to do was wait.

It was time for lunch and they started, followed by the sheriff, toward the bar. They ate sandwiches. After the meal they returned to the office, Just as they entered an agent met them.

- Sheriff, we got a message from Mrs Nora's children, it seems she's not answering the phone, they want us to go and see what happened to her.

- Well go then, What are you waiting for? – Said Zilosky. The man went out followed by another agent.

The FBI agents sat down to examine the situation:- So, by summing it up, the doctor and his girlfriend are fleeing from the police and maybe by someone else. We don't know where they are and we don't even know if they are still alive. Kate, you got news of the man killed?

- Yes, Chief, they have identified him, he is a small half-note criminal belonging to the Jo Laganà clan of Chicago.

- Fuck, him too? The witnesses are from the Laganà clan and also the killed man belongs to that asshole Jo. They are up to something, I don't know what but they are trying to pull the wool over our eyes, but this time I'm going to incriminate that asshole, I swear to God.

They continued making guesses and assumptions for some time, Then Pat's phone rang, it was his wife.

- For God's Sake, how often do I have to tell you that you don't have to call me at work? Of course, as soon as I come back I promise you that we're going on that freaking holiday but now I can't stay on the phone!

"That woman is really Impossible, "he thought.

The office phone rang. The sheriff took the handset and as he listened he nodded, then put it down. He paused for a moment with his eyes lowered, then raised them and with a broken voice from the emotion, he said, "They found Nora with her throat slit in her house with the dog, he's throat was slit too... There were some clothes that seemed to be of two fugitives ... That woman was a good person. What was the need to kill her? She would never hurt anyone, what kind of monster can do this? Nora's truck is gone - then he wiped a tear from his right eye.

"Fuck, then those two are not innocent, they're murderers. But why kill the old lady, they could tie her up if they needed the pickup, why hurt her? From the doctor's profile he did not look like a violent person and the woman was an esteemed university lecturer. No, something does not sound right, but these are the facts for now, "thought the FBI agent.

"Let's go," he said, headed towards the door, - issue a stop order of the van in all neighboring states.

They came to the house in just over an hour, the sight that came before them was scary, blood everywhere. Nora was stretched across the carpet, which was soaked with blood and a stain stretched out in the form of a moon. The head of the old woman almost detached from the neck, numerous knife wounds all over the body. The dog, not far away, had a wound that came from his throat to his chest, completely open as if someone had taken it from the edges and pulled with his hands.

"But what kind of beasts are the ones who committed this crime, why rage against a poor old woman and her dog? They are only beasts, beasts! "

The sheriff ran out in the veranda to vomit, consoled by Agent Kate. Special Agent Blake took the phone out of his pocket but there was no signal, then put it back and came over to the house phone and asked, "Sheriff, it's time to get a hold of yourself. We have a lot of work to do. From where did your men call since the cell phone has no signal? Please tell me they did not use the phone...

The sheriff, still embarrassed, with swollen eyes coming out of the orbits and with the taste of vomit, called an agent and asked him if they had used the fixed telephone. To the affirmative answer of these, Blake took him by the jawbone of his jacket and almost lifted it from the ground.

- You dickhead, have they not taught you to not touch anything in the scene of a crime? From where do you fucking come, idiot? - He barked into his face.

The annihilated agent stammered that he used gloves.

- That does not make you less of a dickhead.

Blake who was one meter and ninety-five tall and weighed 120 Kg was an imposing black man with the crumpled nose that denoted a past of punches taken and given, he put the agent on the floor and shouted:

- Fast, call forensics.

Chapter 24

The truck picked up and spun but for the moment it went. It did not do more than 60 miles per hour but had no cuts, he had full fuel, instead of taking the road that would take them to Prairie City when they arrived on the main street they turned south, they had to take the streets they had decided at Nora's. The old woman had also given him a road map, and now they used that. They took the S6G road and then after a few kilometers they turned right and took the F70, this was straight and misty road with nothing to the right and nothing to the left, stretches of fields interspersed by large and small forests, they encountered some rare dwelling that looked like they were uninhabited. The landscape was as monotonous as it was the annoying the truck, they would soon have to turn and they would have to stop, they needed to buy a cell phone.

- Alan, why are they looking for us?. Who can be interested in what you have discovered? They appear to be gangsters using typical gang methods.

- They want me, I'm the only one who knows how to make the project.

- Now, also Professor Ross knows, - she said.

- Not exactly, in the USB you sent, I've included all the procedures and formulas ... except an important bit, a conjunction ring without which the formulas can't be used.

- Why did you do it? she asked shocked.

- I could not be sure that Ross was not involved, so I kept it as a last resort. From what I sent they can trace back the exact procedure but it will take years of testing.

- But who do you think they are?

- I have no idea. I've been thinking about it all the time but I can't imagine who they might be, including the emissary.

They went on silent. They arrived to Omaha and entered the city avoiding the center. At the first electronics store they stopped and bought a disposable cell phone, Then, always remaining on the periphery, they found a café with a gas station. They got gas and entered in the dining room, sat down at a table and ordered lunch. As they waited, Alan called Ross and informed him of the latest facts and asked if the pen-drive had arrived. The professor replied that it was not yet in his hands, he was in a small village and the mail did not arrive daily..

When they finished eating they went on their way. They took another secondary road, the next stop would be Rising City or some other nearby place to stay. Sara was driving while Alan slept. he had always had the ability to sleep in every place and in every situation, it was a way to recover the strength and it was even a weapon. The rest could be considered preparatory to a fit body and lack of sleep affected the cognitive and physical abilities.

He woke up after an abundant hour and started cleaning the gun, the landscape was even more monotonous if possible. Fields only fields and fields, no houses nor forests or hills, a flat and repetitive plain. From the radio of the van came a country music, monotonous as well, they had not met a car in their path; in sight there was a small gathering of trees.

- Stop at those trees," he said to Sara.

She stopped and he went down, headed behind a tree because he needed to pee, as he went back and saw in the distance a car that was going their same way. "Thanks to God, we are not alone," he thought, and got back in the car.

Chapter 25

Davis was preparing to meet the General Clifford. His hands and armpits were sweating. He knew in his heart that this was his last chance, if he did well, instead if things went bad then he was fucked,. He has been waiting for an hour, he had drank three coffees from the vending machine and each one was more disgusting than the previous one. Despite the morning shower and the deodorant he had put on, he knew he smelled of sweat, which mixed with the cologne he usually carried, made a vomiting mix. Finally, a young lady who would not have disfigured on Playboy's pages, let him in the general's room. After the conveniences of rite the general came immediately to the point.

- What news do you have for me, Davis? I can't wait anymore, you do understand that they also make pressure on me, and if you don't bring me something the first head that will fall will be mine, but I'll take you down with me.

- General, I'm aware of it – Davis said, with the air of the cat getting ready to catch a mouse, he had a winning card but had to play it well, very well. "I don't hide that we have had difficulties, the engine that is being developed is too powerful and it always breaks, if I were to say that we are close to a solution, I would lie ..." he paused and took a sip of water from the glass. - But ... there is a but!

The general was crouched with his squeezed eyes reduced to two heavenly crevices, His skin formed a hollow between the forehead and the nose, the wrinkles of the forehead, accentuated, formed waves, the foreboding of a sea that began to storm, he said nothing..

Davis thought it might be enough: "The interesting news is that we are close to creating a system that moves objects from one side to the other with a minimum energy usage at an awesome speed. Think of the possible implications, moving troops and equipment from one side of the globe to another in a moment, hit the enemy then flee and go back in a flash, and hit back. These are just the possibilities for military use, think in the civil field all the possible applications, people who can move from New York to London in a second at the price of a coffee, the rest I leave to your imagination.

The general relaxed his eyes, now that he was not corroded, two round balls came back, he scratched an ear, and said, "And this thing is real or just in your imagination? Because if its real then you need to get me the procedure, if it is another of your fake news, I advise you to disappear from my presence and not to be seen again.

- In a day we will have the formulas and the procedure, I will give you everything, but I expect the non-military part to remain in my hand with the assurance that I will be able to exploit the trade rights of this discovery without fearing that you intervene to block everything.

- Okay, you have my word, but if tomorrow it's not all in my hands, I will make your life a living hell, keep it in mind.

- Do not doubt it, you will have it.

He left the building as his cellphone rang.

Chapter 26

Professor Ross ended the conversation he had with Alan and was preparing to make a call when the doorbell rang. He went to open, it was a courier who delivered him a packet and he signed the receipt.

He opened the package and went to the computer. In the package there was a USB key with no document attached, he inserted the key into the computer and opened it, inside there were many documents and pictures. He opened the first document and read, meanwhile the old red-and-white cat was sitting on his legs and fused, he caressed him. He read more lines, "Really genial, very ingenious, I was not wrong about that guy, he is really good, there's nothing to say, "then took the phone and dialed a number.

Chapter 27

The car, which went their same way, came close. Alan felt the hair of his neck rise and stood up, looked in the mirror, Sara noticed his agitation, and asked, "What's happening, what did you see?"

- A car is behind us, I don't know why but I feel we can't stay calm, you continue to drive

By now the car was about 50 meters away and was approaching quickly, Alan recalled it was same model as the one that had tried to spur them and made them fall into the river, and with vigilant senses he opened the window.

- If they do something wrong, do it immediately as I say.

The car did not go any further, it was always at a constant distance. The fields were leaving room for groups of trees and the road began to have some curves. The pursuers disappeared at every turn to reappear afterwards, but they did not come near.

They went on like this for quite a while. The truck crashed and rumbled, screaming and trembling but continued its march undaunted, the car got closer, now it had increased its speed.

He hated being paranoid, maybe they were going to surpass them, but something told him that was not the case, the car was ten meters away.

From the mirror he saw the passenger leaning out of the window holding a gun

- Sara, stay down and drive zig zag, they're gonna shoot us - as he spoke these words, a shot hit the back of the van, maybe it was just a warning shot.

Looking in the mirror he saw that there were three passengers , the one who was driving was part of the assailants in the woods and it was the basset, the guy who fired was Quadro and the other he did not see well because he was in the back seat but he did not seem to know him. So they were the same people in the forest, he knew they were dangerous :they had already killed.

Another shot came from the chasing car and hit the outside mirror of the driver's seat. Sara shouted, he had to react, he did not want to kill but he had to defend herself. he leaned out of the window and fired two shots that did not hit them, he aimed at the tires but missed them. Quadro responded to the fire and a bullet passed dangerously close to his head, he retreated.

- Now when I tell you you move all the left, stay a while and then get back to the right.

Nearby there was a curve they ran at full speed, just past it Alan shouted to Sara: - Now!

The van moved and while the car was in view he began to shoot, this time aiming at the engine and windshield of the car trying to hit the driver. He unloaded the gun, inserted a new charger and continued to fire.

The chasing car came closer, but when he fired it moved away again making it difficult to hit the target. He finished the shots and reloaded the gun, at that moment a shred of shots hit the truck, he leaned out of the window and fired. He fired a shot and aimed at the target again, then fired aiming the bullets at the men who were chasing him.

The car that followed slammed to avoid the shots, the first burst broke down on the windshield, shattering it, but a bullet had stuck in the neck of the third occupant who was now shouting with shrieking cries while trying in vain to tampon the open wound in his neck. a red sketch had smudged everything. The blood continued to pour out, at each pump of the heart, other sketches hit the other occupants and the seats.

The driver, to see the road, had stuck his head out of the window, the second burst shot by Alan caused the radiator to break. A white smoke puff came out of the bonnet of the car that followed them and the car approached to the side and then stopped.

- How did they find us? She said.

- I have no idea, But someone must have warned them, But I cannot understand how they knew we were on a van. Anyway, I think I hit one of them.

They went on, silently, they were frightened

- In the next town we will separate, I can't risk your life, you have nothing to do with this, you just have the misfortune of being with me.

- That's out of the question.- she replied.

- Listen to me Sara, if you're with me my moves are limited, it's no longer a game, we are risking our lives and I don't want to risk yours. If I know you're not in danger I'm stronger and then you can be more useful to me for other things, you alone will have more freedom of movement and me too.

Sara was not very convinced. - Alan, I love you and if something happens to you ...

- I love you too Sara and that's why I don't want you at risk, do you trust me?

65

- Yes, but I'm so scared for you.

- If you trust me I have a plan, I have to understand who these people are and I can do better if you are not there. As soon as you can, go back to South Band and go to the police.

Alan told her he plan he had devised.

Chapter 28

Rocco, all smeared with blood, got out of the car.

- Shit, shit, shit a thousand times, that asshole has managed to escape also this time. Is he dead?

- Stuck like a salt cod, he was hit at jugular, he had no escape, - said Quadro.

- Now we have to hide the corpse, then I'll call my father.

They dragged the body into the thick of a grove. They did not have the means to dig a pit, so they covered his body with rocks, then hid them with leaves and branches. For now it could be enough but the body would be discovered and they should be far away. Now they had to take care of the car. With a tremendous effort they dragged the car into the woods, hiding it, covered it with branches, removed the plates, and buried them away, then Rocco picked up the phone and called his father. He listened almost without talking, then told him what had happened, then interrupted the conversation.

- We have new orders, now those two are no longer untouchable, we have to kill them -he said with a grin.

Chapter 29

Nathan was out of the shelter to smoke, it was an old workshop in disuse, had a large central hall with iron beams, all rusty; The drops of water fell from the ceiling which in some places was dim and brought in the light of day. On the concrete floor there were oil stains, grease and oil formed iridescent arabesques when they were affected by sunlight, they were like fractals, the mold had invaded the room, and some outer branches began to peep off the crevices that opened, soon the nature would take over the place once again.

The scientists were locked up in what they once had to be the offices. He and Erwin slept in a small room where they had the equipment to record images and voices. The phone rang, it was Laganà, he listened quietly nodding then he called Erwin.

–   I have to go into town. They're sending two more people so we can take a break, the orders are changed now we can also kill them if they will not do as we say, I will be away for two or three hours. Try not to mess anything up.

- Go, boss, don't worry - Erwin grinned.

Nathan walked to the car and started lifting a cloud of dust.

Chapter 30

Once alone, Erwin rubbed his hands and sinful thoughts crossed his mind, that woman made him go crazy, those swollen breasts and those torn legs caused him erotic dreams and nighttime erections. More than once he had been masturbating in the bathroom thinking of her, he seemed to be a little kid like when his mother locked him in the bedroom while she was "working," she heard her moan and shout, and he could not help but masturbate. Then he tried to limit the squirt that spurted out of his penis because his mother would get angry if she found the blankets dirty and then she'd beat him and would not allow him out of his room for days. He had never known his father. With a good chance her father was one of her mom's friends, despite her working a lot, they had many economic difficulties, the

67

woman spent almost everything on drugs and there was little and nothing to eat or dress.

When he was 16, he escaped and lived in expeditions like a homeless, robbing pedestrians and old people, He was not scrupulous, if they did not give up immediately, he would beat them up, not caring for the pain he caused. His vice were the whores, consuming the act violently, as if in each one of them he saw the figure of his mother and wanted her to pay for everything he had suffered, he often beat and robbed them.

He continued with this kind of life until he was 22 years old, then one day a half-note trader who he counted among his "friends" told him that there was a Chicago band that was looking for valued men without fear. He went to Laganà's home before his friend's phone call, and he had started to work with him. The early days had been silent and good trying to learn the job from the more experienced ones, with time he had gotten a reputation of hard and unscrupulous that had integrated him well in the gang. He was not very clever and this prevented his possible ascendancy into the malevolent hierarchies, but he was trustworthy. Every task that was assigned to him he did it without discussing it and this had given him some respect in those environments.

He headed for the dungeon, he had a half erection already, and he anticipated what would happen in a short while, he was so excited that he forgot to put his cap on.

Chapter 31

Professor Ross went to the kitchen and prepared a tuna sandwich, then took the bowl of crisps and poured it a bit to feed the cat, he had spent several hours on Alan's notes and formulas but still could not understand neither the formulas nor the applied equations. There was something wrong with him. That guy was a genius so if he had found the way he would have succeeded too, but he could not see the right path, he would have to work all night, but he was used to it.

When he taught at Notre Dame sometimes, to solve a problem, he took more nights, during those forced vigils he drank a staggering amount of coffee, black and strong. His students appreciated him for his silly way of expounding complex theories, and they appreciated the simplicity with which he displayed mathematical equations and functions; Explained by him even the toughest things appeared to everyone's reach. He wanted to become Dean of the university but every time there was someone who overcame him, for one reason or another he always came at the wrong time in the wrong place.

His ambitions were continually discouraged, he did not feel appreciated for what he was. His wife understood well his mood and, when she saw him agitated, she could always calm him down. She was his tranquilizer, his safe shelter from the bitterness of life. Along with her, he had had a full life with a son he loved. But he too had disappointed him, had married a dry woman whom he did not like. He had a grandson but he seldom saw him . But, in the background, he had always kept this suffering of the lack of recognition of his abilities.

Then she died and without his salvation he had been lost, at first he had thought of continuing the research by moving closer to his son to be close to him and staying near his grandson, but then the disagreements with his daughter-in-law, had convinced him that it was not the case. In the end he had resigned himself, the few publications he had produced had not saved him from academic anonymity and the hopes of becoming famous in his environment were scarce, almost null, without the machines and without comparison it was difficult to obtain results. When he finished eating he went back to the computer, it would be a long night.

Chapter 32

Pat Blake answered the phone, it was his wife, he listened to what she had to say, her son had quarreled with a mate at school and was punched in the eye, that it was all black, he was losing patience. He should have made it clear to that woman that he was not a salesman and when he was at work he could not be disturbed except for "really" urgent things; He rebuked his wife once again and cut the conversation short. The sheriff was coming holding a paper in his hand.

- Agent, they found a corpse and a hidden car. A hunter with the dog passed by that area when the dog started barking and brought him close to a rudimentary tomb made of a bunch of stones.

- Well, let's go there.

They arrived there as forensics was already doing their job, even the coroner had already arrived. Agent Blake turned to the coroner:

- Doctor, what can you tell me?

The doctor was a low, thin man with two square goggles too large for him, he continually scratched his chin as if he had a three-day beard. In reality he had a little hair on his face who he showed off proudly, in front of Pat it looked like a dwarf.

- The corpse belongs to a man of the apparent age of 30-35 years, he was hit at the juggler by a bullet and died in a few minutes. The death was more or less four hours ago, - the doctor said.

The FBI agent thanked him. At a rapid pace, he went a little further away where the car had been hidden, a forensics agent was detecting the fingerprints.

- Have you already identified the chassis number? - He asked.

- Yes I wrote down it on this paper - he gave it to Pat.

He picked it up and immediately called the station, after a short wait, they told him that the car belonged to a Chicago company that was linked to Jo Laganà. "Bingo" he thought, "we'll wait for the corpse's fingerprints, and then we'll see."

Chapter 33

When they arrived at Omaha, they left the highway 92 and took the junction that would take them to town. They stopped at a fuel station where they bought a phone for Sara, then headed to Eppley Airport where they left the old van in long-term parking.

- Do you really want us to separate? She asked while separating the few remaining dollars.

- We'll keep in touch via phone. Near here I have a friend, I will try to reach him, you do as we agreed.

They looked at each other. for a long time, both aware that it could be the last time and they exchanged a warm and long kiss. They headed to the airport to buy the ticket. Alan left her in the waiting room, she looked at him from the window until he disappeared.

Once alone, a bunch of thoughts crowded his mind, now he was alone, really alone, and he had to look for help. He thought of his friend Bill. It was years since he last heard from him, he hoped that he still lived in the same place. He also thought that he might have done better to turn to the police but did not trust them all the way, he was not sure that by turning to them he would find someone willing to listen to his version of the facts, maybe they would have sent him directly to jail, but who knows maybe that would be the best solution, but he was now in Nebraska. He was getting close to Ross's house

He called a taxi and went to a used car dealer. After calculating the dollars he had in his pocket, he chose a used BMW but it seemed good and did not cost much. Shortly after, he hit the road. His friend Bill lived in Denver, Colorado, he had to make a south deviation, he did not know if he still lived in the same place, did not have his phone number in the cell phone he had bought and did not remember it by heart, he decided however to try. It was late afternoon and he should have stayed somewhere down the road. He came to North Platte, a dingy town with almost all single-story buildings; By now the sun was setting and sending golden reflections on houses and trees, the neon signs were beginning to light up, he saw a motel with a restaurant on the opposite side of the road and decided to stop for the night.

Chapter 34

The door opened with a squeak, the low and crude individual came in. "Robin," Martin thought, he had the gun in his hand, stopped at the door, scrutinizing them and smiling. He was a disgusting individual. The incipient baldness made the round face look like a billiard ball, black and big booby eyes, one of them squinting, stained teeth like some northern African for excessive use of turmeric and low hygiene in washing. He had a rough three-day beard, his cheeks were asymmetrical, one lower than the other, and made the face less round than it was. But his squinting eyes and unclear cheekbones helped form a grotesque face with an expression of wickedness, Erwin grinned and a drooled.

- Nice lady, you have to come with me.

- Out of the question. She is not going anywhere - Ortiz said indignantly, realizing what the individual had in mind.

- little man, who was talking to you? He asked, advancing with the gun pointed at them and heading toward Mary.

Ortiz became angry with rage and indignation, a dormant frustration, He knew that he should not do anything reckless, but he could not help it, he got up up like a spring, and with a leap he tried to jump on the bandit, but Erwin caught sight of his intentions, fired and stopped his aggressor, the bullet crossed the left biceps, Mary screamed.

Pain ran through Ortiz's body and mind, light flashed through his brain, and every lightning was accompanied by a shock of pain, he fell on the bed and did not move anymore.

- Anyone else wants to try? I still have several bullets and you are no longer a rare commodity, now I can even kill you all.

He took Mary by an arm and raised her from her bunk. she fluttered furiously, Erwin slapped her so hard that she fell back on the bed. The woman wiped away a rush of blood, then spit. She felt a mix of disgust and repugnance for that crude and wicked individual. "If I don't obey, this beast is capable of killing us all."

- Okay, I'll do what you want - she said in a whisper.

- No Mary, don't do it, - Martin cried.

- Be quiet, otherwise I'll shoot you too, be good and the lady will be fine, in fact ... - and dragging Mary out of the room he left.

- We should not have let that happen, we're four against one, - said Freddy, who until then had not said one word.

- Yes, but he has a gun and we don't, - Martin said.

In the meantime, Ortiz had recovered and held his arm with his hand trying to stop the bleeding, the other two friends tried to buffer the wound with stripes taken from their shirts.

- As soon as he comes back we must be ready and attack him, we must flee from here, here is what we're going to do - Martin exposed what he thought was a good plan.

Erwin had taken Mary screaming by her hair and dragged her toward the room where he slept with Nathan.

- Be silent, bitch, no one can hear you, we're going to have fun, then you'll thank me - he threw her down on the bed and pulled off her blouse.

She tried to rebel, scream and scratch him every time she could, but he was too strong. He slapped her again and then after he punched, Mary stopped fighting. The man took off her skirt and turned her around He held her with one hand while with the other he loosened his belt and lowered his pants. He penetrated her with animal violence, she screamed as her tearful tears came down her cheeks. She felt His warm breath On the neck and the saliva, that was flowing from his mouth, slip into her hand; He thought of Jeff then everything went dark and for her luck she passed out..

Chapter 35

Nathan arrived at the venue where he was supposed to meet with the other accomplices, and he parked the car far away. During the trip he had thought of a possible escape from that situation that had become dangerous but had not found any kind of solution, he had to continue the game. It was too important. If he were to fail they would kill him without pity, he knew this, but he also knew that he wanted to return as soon as possible to his girlfriend Linda. When they had separated, he had told her that he had to go abroad for work and did not know how long he would have been gone

It could be two or three months, they would talk on the phone, but not so often since the communications were difficult, he had added nothing more. Linda was used to these situations, he never talked about work, told her he was working for a government body and could not talk about what he was doing. He had met her during a party from some common friends, they liked each other. He knew that with his job to have a fixed relationship would be problematic, but he did not resist to that girl full of life and good humor. While these thoughts thronged his mind he entered the room and approached the counter.

- It's not very cold for the season, – he told the bartender the agreed word. He poured him a scotch and pointed to a door at the bottom of the room with a nod of his head. He entered the room, there was a pool table and tables with chairs, at one of these tables were seated two corpulent men with their shirts pulling on prominent abdomens. "Beer drinkers," he thought. In fact the two men had two beer mugs still half full and they were talking to each other. As soon as they saw him, the eldest of the two made a nod with his head inviting him to sit down.

- Nice to meet you, I'm John, - said the older one.
- You can call me Smith, - said the other man.

John, in reality, was called Bill Dawson and it was Jo Laganà's right arm, he was a hired killer, Ruthless and unscrupulous.

He had met him during a dinner at Jo's house. That night around the table were gathered all the heads of the senior staff and Jo had introduced Nathan to the other diners. He kept a low profile, had recently entered the malevolent organization and preferred not to show off. They were discussing a huge amount of drug that had to come from Canada through Lake Michigan and They were arranging sorting and storage. He listened attentively to the organizational arrangements, but he did not say a word..

He had been struggling to gain Jo's confidence, his job would go on for a long time, but he had a shot of luck. One day he had the job of accompanying Jo's daughter shopping, the girl was a sixteen bizarre and even ugly girl, annoying as hunger, it was clear that she had grown up in a cocoon. Every her desire became order and the girl loved this, she controlled Jo's men, Who loved his daughter, in contrast to his son Rocco whom he judged an incapable.

They had to go to a luxury shopping mall where the cheapest shop was a boutique, on the way he realized that a car followed them, he had taken secondary roads and done different turns to make sure he was not wrong. Whenever he was on a side street, the girl scolded him with arrogance, he told her to be good because a car was following them, then the girl called her father. Once at the parking of the shopping center they rushed out of the car to get into a crowded place where they would be relatively safe.

Once out of the car, the men in the car had started to fire, he had lowered the girl and had responded to the fire; A bullet had stuck in one arm but had continued to shoot by killing two aggressors while the girl was lying on the floor and trembling like a leaf. He had kept the assailants down until Jo's men had arrived and had taken care of the situation. The men belonged to a rival band and had tried to kidnap or kill the daughter of the boss.

Nathan's gesture gained Jo's unconditional confidence and his gratitude. From then on his task was much easier, he was entrusted important missions and made him participate in the most important meetings, his salary had much increased and the benefits were of another category. So he had already met John or Bill. He had pretended not to know him or did not recognize him and he played along. The older man who appeared to be the boss also said that they had been sent to strengthen the surveillance and not to give him and Erwin a break and that he had to lead them to the place where the scientists were held. Nathan got up guiding them to the car. "The situation is even more complicated," if Erwin could not be a problem, these two would make things much worse. They headed for the refuge.

Chapter 36

Sara took the first flight home, she looked forward to taking a shower and change clothes, those last hours had exhausted her, she had not heard from Alan anymore. The whole story flashed before her eyes, she was not accustomed to those events, She was a quiet teacher not a secret agent. She remembered the fall in the river and the nice old lady Nora who had been so kind to them, the trip with the grungy van and the gunfire along the road.

Alan had behaved as if he were used to such events, she knew he had been in the Marines but she did not think he was so skilled even with firearms. When this whole story would be over, she would no longer let him run away from her. She dreamed a life with him, with children and Sunday barbecues with friends, In short, a quiet and normal life next to the man she loved. While her thoughts wandered, her attention fell on Alan's discovery, according to what he had explained to her, the phenomenon that appeared under the glass bell was inexplicable, it worked but he did not know what made it work.

Certainly once he understood the principle it could be a Nobel worthy discovery. She imagined him with the tuxedo and the bow tie and she laughed, everyone complimenting him and ready to shake his hand and a row of industries ready to buy the patent. He would have tons of money. His invention would revolutionize the world, the possibilities were infinite and she lost herself in listing all the applications that came to her mind.

Sara Dixon was born in a small town near Indianapolis, Greenfield, in the Hangcock County; Her father was employed in an insurance company while her mother was a housewife and painted. She had a sister ten years younger than her , Gloria, who was currently attending college in Indianapolis. She still remembered when she was an adolescent, almost a woman, and her sister still a little girl, swimming in the pool outside the house, which her father had wanted for them, located in the garden of the house where they lived during those hot Indiana summers. When they were swimming, they would play jokes on each other and they pulled each other's hair, they held the brunt for a while, and then laughed like crazy.

She had had a happy and serene childhood, Her deeply Catholic parents made her to go to church every Sunday and even forced her to enter the church chorus. She liked to sing, she had a melodious voice, but she did not like to sing those church songs, she preferred Mariah Carey's music, she only enjoyed it when at Christmas she sang "*All I Want For Christmas Is You*". With these thoughts in her head, the journey was very short.

As soon as she landed she headed for the exit, looked around to see if there was anything strange or someone who followed her but saw no one, called a cab to go home. The landscape flowed softly and she wrapped herself in those thoughts that had filled her mind while on the plane; The driver's voice, who informed her that they had arrived at destination and the price of the race, woke her up. She opened the house door and walked inside..

Immediately a smell of stale smoke and decomposing food assaulted her; "What happened? The fridge must be broken ", The smell was everywhere, an acrid smell attacked her nostrils. She entered the kitchen, dozens of beer cans were scattered around the floor, the smoking table in front of the couch was flooded with plastic dishes and containers for takeaway food, pizza cartons were leaning against the counter of the kitchen, Scared she turned around to leave the house but a strong hand stuck her mouth as a rag fell on her nose, she only had the time to think that they were waiting for her when she lost her senses.

Chapter 37

Pat Blake cursed at himself, no news came in, he waited for the phone ring anytime now to know who the fingerprints found in the car belonged to.

Meanwhile, he had put a team on Jo's heels, sooner or later he would have made a false step, but until then he behaved normally as if he were the most candid of souls, a citizen who respected laws and institutions. But Pat knew he was a bastard son of a bitch, everyone knew that but, until that moment, they had not found any prof, it was at least two years since he had started trying all sorts of ways, stakeouts, phones under control but that individual was too cunning.

When he spoke on the phone he generally talked about golf, his favorite sport, he spoke of green and bats, It was clear that he was referring to something else but they did not have any evidence, every time they tried to catch him red-handed he ended up being always clean, maybe someone in the police was working for him.

Even the DEA, with which Pat worked intensively, was unable to find evidence about him and so they decided to change the method since the traditional one did not work. He stretched out his legs and leaned on another chair, he was not a bon ton champion, he blasphemed, drank, smoked and sometimes played but he was a good cop and a good father, except when work had to be done, which was basically almost always, but he loved his job and maybe spent more time on it than with the family.

The Sheriff approached him with the cordless in his hand: "Agent, a call for you from the station," he said, handing him the phone.

- Blake, - he said, listening. While he was listening, he nodded with his head creaked now with some gray hair.

After the call was over he called the sheriff. - The fingerprints belong to Rocco Laganà and Dave Patterson who belongs to the family, issue a capture warrant and put their credit cards under control.

"Well something is starting to move," he thought as he relaxed and scratched his calf.

Kate Ball stretched out to him a cup of coffee, took it to his lips and drank a long sip, then snorted out: "Puah Kate, fuck!

You know I like it sweet, this is as bitter as the bile- he murmured.

- Sorry, boss, I forgot the sugar, "said the agent, smiling

"The boss is SO cool, scary, but as a cop he has two big balls!" She thought, "Shit, I'm going to start talking like him now."

Chapter 38

Erwin, not much satisfied, buttoned his fly, that bitch had not given him much satisfaction, she shouted for a while, she moved but just a little, then she turned silent and remained motionless. When they did so, he did not like them much, he liked it when they moved and begged him to stop, when they shouted and scratched like angry cats, he really enjoyed himself then, but with her he could not even come, he would have had to masturbate .

- Come on, beauty, It's time to go back to the pen - he said, taking her by the arm and raising her. She did not react, her eyes were barred, fixed, the eyelids lowered, but rarely, the gaze lost in the void.

- Don't play with me, hon, I did not hurt you, I just wanted to have fun together, - he said worried about her state, he dragged her hard, she followed docile but did not react, she seemed like a drug addict, or like she had ingested too many tranquilizers.

"If something happened to her, they'll make me pay for it. When Nathan returns, I'll tell him that I found her like this. "

He walked to the prison dragging the woman who traversed her feet. He took the key and put it in the keyhole, turned it, opened the door and pushed her inside while he himself was about to enter with the gun in his fist. He was halfway in, being preceded by the gun, when the door closed with a tremendous hit that broke at least two of his ribs, but he still held the gun in his hand. He was stuck, breathing hard, a steel arm closed around his neck, the door clamped him like a vice grip. At each lap of the vise grip the chest pain increased of intensity, he tried to shoot at his aggressor but could not force the trigger, Finally he managed to shoot, but the bullet planted in the wall. Martin had grabbed the bandit around his neck and shook him with all his scary force.

- don't let the door go, push harder, we have to crush this bastard," he yelled at the other two who, snorting, stood behind the door and were pushing Erwin with all their strength.

- Push, push,- Martin continued.

By now, he too sweated sweepingly and the drops of sweat came down his red hair and fell on his neck and eyes, which were now burning, but he continued to tighten the bandit's neck with all the strength he had. Anger multiplied his strength, the bandit snorted and twirled, turned the eyes, now there was only white, the pupils were gone but he kept holding tight until he felt a *crack*!

He did not let go, so Freddy shouted at him, - Stop Martin, Stop, he's dead, leave him!

He recovered and loosened his grip, he had short breath, wiped his sweat with one hand, and only then did he realize: "My God I killed a man, what did I do? I did not want to, I did not ...

Gustavo Ortiz put his hand on his shoulder and he let his friend sit down. "You've been forced my friend, it was either him or us, you did good Martin, this bandit belonged to the human scum, he did not deserve to live, now we can run away. Come on, let's take care of Mary, she does not look good to me.

Martin recovered but he still did not believe that he, a man so gentle, so agreeable and lover of the quiet life, had killed a man. Gustavo took the reins of the situation, pulled his friends out, grabbed the gunman's gun, and put it in his belt, told Freddy to retrieve food, gave a little water to Mary, and pushed everyone out of the shed .

It was already dark outside, with the sky crossed by some red streaks, the night was lukewarm, a chorus of crickets and a sound of frogs welcomed them, a distant owl shouted loudly.

- Where do we go now? Martin said - We don't know where we are, we can't see anything and we don't have a torch.

- From that side I hear a river and I seem to see trees, let's go there,- Freddy suggested.

Martin led the way as Freddy dragged behind Mary and Gustavo closed the row, always with the gun in his hand.

They came to the river, the water flowing placid and dark, more than a river it looked like a brook. It was about five feet wide but it had to be deep. There was a pale moon that illuminated slightly, but the fog was rising, it could be good if they were looking for them but it was a bad thing for them since they could not see where to go. There was no light in the surroundings, they had to hurry up and get someplace safe. Walking along the embankment they found a shaky wooden bridge crossing the river, on the other side they saw the trees, it could be a wood, they could have found a better hiding place there.

They crossed the bridge and came to the opposite creek, after a few meters there was actually a forest, they entered it with difficulty, the trees were dense and a compact undergrowth bush prevented the movements, some spiny bushes made it harder to walk since they planted their thorns in their dress stopping their advance, until they were torn off. A few meters ahead the woods became more rude and the way forward became easier..

- That is the polar star, - said Gustavo, - in which direction do we go, in your opinion?

- I don't know, but my favorite point is the north, - said Freddy, - so let's go north

The decision was taken but the friends did not know that if they had instead gone south they would have found the highway not too far from where they were. They walked north, which was the opposite direction from which they came, walked for about an hour, dragging behind Mary who was always catatonic and did not respond to any stimulus. Once they found in a clearing they decided to stop to rest and refresh themselves with the food they had brought along, they had not gone a long way.

- Do you think they will chase us? - Freddy said to the other two.

— You bet they will, replied Gustavo, – so now we rest for ten minutes and then we resume the journey, we don't know where we are going but they don't know what direction we have taken, certainly with Mary in these conditions we can't go much far.

Chapter 39

Nathan drove thoughtfully while smoking with the window slightly open to let the smoke out, the other two men were chatting to each other as if they were on a pleasure trip. They were almost at destination and he really hoped that Erwin was good and calm; by now he knew him well and knew he was a violent psychopath but he also knew that he usually followed instructions and this time they had been clear, Erwin feared and respected Laganà, so even if worried, he was pretty sure that nothing had gone wrong.

As soon as they arrived at the shed they got out of the car and went inside, a strange silence reigned and Nathan's concern became more pronounced. He take out the gun from the holster, cautiously went to the prison room, after turning the corner he saw the open door and the feet of a man lying on the ground with his distorted legs. He advanced cautiously and put his head inside the cell ... empty! The body stretched to the ground was Erwin's, his neck turned in an unnatural position, his tongue out of his teeth, and with cuts on it as if he had bit it with violence, his were eyes wide open and his irises were barely visible. "If he was ugly, now he's horrible," he thought, walking into the room. He nodded with the gun to the other men to inspect the rest of the shed in silence, the men turned away cautiously. He checked the room, there were no sign of struggle, then he saw the bullet hole on the wall, obviously they had attacked him, but why did he enter the room? The orders were accurate. When he got out he headed to the place where he and Erwin usually slept and ate, the others came out with a nod to say that there was no one around.

- They can't have gone too far, we have to find them,- he said, guiding the others.

Outside the shed they looked around, they could have gone in the direction of the main road or in the direction of the forest, most probably the road, the rest were mostly cultivated fileds,where they could not hide.

- Let's go, I think they headed for the woods, we have to find them, but they could also have gone towards the road, so we have to separate.

- You check the main road, Nathan and I will go to the woods, the first one who finds them call others, - said John or Bill, unfortunately there was no cellphone signal there.

They walked toward the river for a short distance, cautiously patrolling the surroundings with guns in hand and an inclined posture, they arrived at the bridge and they stopped to listen, but they only head the nocturnal animals that had come to life, the moon was now high in the sky but the fog confused the contours of things and made it difficult to distinguish details, a dense smoke rose from the river.

They crossed the bridge that squeaked fearfully under their feet, once they arrived on the other side they stopped to listen again. In front of them the wood was dense, to the right and left the river was flowing about ten meters from the woods. They could have gone in any direction, perhaps the less likely direction was just north, there the woods were dense, and those who were all but explorers, yet they had shown courage and inventiveness considering they were able to kill Erwin, so if the less likely direction was north, they would go north.

Chapter 40

They all sat silently with their thoughts, Mary had a blank stare, and did not say a word, Freddy near her was trying to awaken her from that comatose state she had fallen in, but the results were null.

Gustavo stood up: - It's time to go, we've rested too much." His face showed a scratch that went from the right eye all the way to the cheek and the mouth.

They walked always toward the north, dragging behind Mary, who dragged her feet. Out of the clearing and just a few feet away, before them came a pathway, it was small but allowed to walk with some ease, they decided to follow it. The road was not straight but it made dry curves to the right and to the left, they walked in silence forming a single line.

- Where do you think we are? Said Gustavo.

- I have no idea, - Martin replied.

They continued to follow the path always in silence; The night around them offered her typical sounds and rustling of animals, The ground was beginning to rise and they were getting more and more fatigued, the wood was shriveled and then suddenly thickened again. Sometimes they stopped while remaining silent to hear any car sounds that indicated the proximity of a road, but it was all silent, except the noise of the woods.

Suddenly a noise, unlike the others, made the blood run cold, they all stopped silently to listen, it sounded like steps. The tension was palpable, Gustavo pulled out the gun and held it in the direction from which the noise came. The steps were approaching, their hearts pounding, only Mary seemed alien to that tension, still lived in her own little world. The noise was near by now and they were all preparing for the worse when a deer with scary horns came towards them. The animal sniffed the air, throwing smoke from the nostrils, it had not seen them.

They stood still and, despite the fear and tension of that moment, they admired the majestic beauty of that inhabitant of the woods, then the deer saw them, snapped to the right, and with a leap disappeared. They looked and breathed a sigh of relief and, always in silence, they resumed their march, following the path. They walked for at least another hour, then the gurgling of flowing water came to their ears.

- I think we're back to the river, - Martin said.

- I don't think so, we've always walked in line with the star, it's more likely that the river has deviated and now runs parallel to us,- Gustavo replied.

They resumed their journey in the direction of the noise, suddenly the sight opened and appeared a mirror of water that was magnifying the moon reflected on the calm surface, they had come to a lake, it was stretched, narrow where they had reached, then it widened. On the right and left of the canal there was always the woods, they decided to walk the left bank where the wood seemed less dense.

They walked all the way to the end of the lake, there was a bridge crossing the emissary and which led to the other side.

- My God, I know where we are," said Freddy, "this is the Crooked Creek Lake, I used to come fish here when I was a child, we are south of Indianapolis a long way away from Bend, around here there is nothing, just woods, but there is a road nearby, we are safe!

They sat down to rest.

Chapter 41

At the sight of the lake the memories of when he was a kid came back to him, his father who was a stubborn fisherman always took him along Freddy did not like fishing, just like he did not enjoy anything his father liked. He liked rugby and he did not, hunting and he did not, fishing and he did not, his father was an obese man who drank beer and ate sausages and burgers as if he was paid, well that was the only thing they had in common. His father was proud of that son who reminded him of when he was young, so he always took him along with him thinking he would enjoy it, Freddy followed him just to avoid disappointing rather than anything else.

He liked to study and for his age, he was very educated, His father was very proud; He had not studied, and whenever that child opened his mouth, all his pride came out of his watery eyes. At school he had always been the first in the class, at ten years he had to put on the glasses, his flaccid appearance, the glasses and a bizarre haircut with the line on one side had contributed to make him the laughing stock of the school, The girls avoided him, and his class mates mocked him and called him a "bunch of lard", he did not care.

The girls left him indifferent, he felt sorry for this classmates, feeling superior. The classmates' attitude changed completely when there was a quiz, then they became friendly, in the early days he did not go help them with cheating on the test, believing that everyone had to fight with their own means, then one day after school, as he was walking home eating a cereal bar, behind a corner waiting for him where four kids, who kicked him and punched for good. When he got home his father was there too,, when he first saw him he hugged him, then started laughing.

- Did you get into a fight? I hope you kicked their asses.

In reality the one who got his ass kicked was him,, but from that day on he would always share his homework. Growing up, his interest in women had increased but not viscerally, he certainly was curious about those round and sinuous bodies, but he found them silly and stupid, making foolish chats and who seemed interested only in boys. After puberty, the curiosity grew again, He felt he wanted them and made erotic dreams, then he would lock himself in the bathroom to unload..

There was Betty who aroused him particularly, she was a girl different from the others, Very smart and not as silly as most friends, but she had the things that everyone else had, put in all the right places. Except that Freddy did not have the courage to declare him when they were together They spoke of math. of physics and other subjects which both were passionate of, but never of love, he struggled but did not know how to do it, he was afraid of her rejection. Then one day Betty moved to another town and he did not see or hear from her anymore.

On the other hand, a new boy came to town, Tom, he was a handsome boy with the bully-like air, all the girls were dying behind him and he took advantage of them, he envied his cockiness. Despite the bully air, Tom liked Freddy and became his best friend, also because at school he was not a great genius and he shared all of his homework and invited him home to study. His friend understood him better than anyone else, took his got his first hangover with him, and he taught him how to smoke, then one day he told him that he had to go some place and asked him to accompany him, he told him to dress well and he picked him up.

He took him in a house with red shades, he submissively followed him, they walked inside and were welcomed by a woman with a transparent gown and without bra with tiny panties that let them glimpse and imagine everything. Freddy stopped salivating and the pulsations of his heart accelerated immediately, He felt his heart beating sharply in his chest, and a heat spread across his face and lower abdomen, he began sweating copiously and could not emit any sound.

- Lilli, meet Freddy, a friend of mine, he needs a push and I know you're good at this kind of thing, I trust you.

- No, no, - he murmured.

But she took him by the hand and led him into a room. It was then that he lost the virginity. Tom took him to Lilli several times, and every time he was always better, then Tom changed city but he had learned the way and went on his own.

Now that he was an adult he learned to appreciate the prostitutes, they did not create any problems, it was enough to pay them and everything was fixed, he had gotten married, and the only platonic love of his youth was the only one, he was comforted with love for dogs, Wolf was the last and most loved one.

Chapter 42

Nathan knew that if they had not made a few false steps, finding them would be extremely difficult, they had gone north but had no idea where they were. They had been walking for two hours on the path they had found, but there was no noise and no trace of the scientists, he decided they would continue a little longer and then they would go back. By now it was almost midnight and the hopes of finding them were thinning.

John followed him silently without protesting. He should have reported to Jo anyway, but the boss would not take it well, it was not his fault obviously, he was not there when they had fled, but to explain that Erwin the psychopath has made a mess was hard; He was under his command and the responsibility was, however, his own. He was absorbed in these thoughts when a terrifying scream broke through the night, it sounded like a wolf, but it was undoubtedly human. The scream stopped suddenly followed immediately by another, if possible even more acute and impressive, like the screaming of the dead who do not want to leave this world.

- Let's go, it's them- he said.

Chapter 43

Once inside the motel he asked for a room for the night, took the money out of his pocket and noticed that there were only a few left, then decided to use the credit card that Sara had left him. Hardly the clerk would look at the name. After paying, he went to the restaurant, walked in and sat down at the far end of the pub near the glass window, where he could keep an eye on the surrounding environment. He ordered omelettes with onions and a Bud and then coffee, he ate, realizing he was hungry, bought a packet of cigarettes and sat out of the place to smoke.

On the nearby road the cars transited at a reduced speed, the traffic was very low, and between one car and the other the singing of the crickets rose sharply, He remembered Nora's house and the moment of tranquility they had. He turned on another cigarette tasting the smell of smoke and breathing in together the smell of the night and the coming spring, the evening was lukewarm. He decided to call Sara. He dialed the home number first but nobody answered, then called the cellphone but it was turned off, he did not worry much and he headed to his room.

He took a refreshing shower and slipped into the bed, realized that he was very tired and shortly afterwards he fell asleep. He slept for a couple of hours when the phone woke him up.

Chapter 44

That night he had to be seen in public, he decided to go to dinner at the usual restaurant where he usually dined. He telephoned to book a table, then left the office. He arrived at the restaurant with ten minutes to eight pm, Usually he ate much later but that night it was essential that he respected the times. The maitre welcomed him with his false smile and made him sit at his usual corner table, An attentive waiter came with his usual favorite drink; In that place they knew him well and, if necessary, there were so many people who could confirm his presence at that hour.

The waiter approached to his table but he kindly dismissed him saying that he should have his drink first. He still wasted time by sipping slowly the amber fluid and making signs to the other tables where his acquaintances sat. "The more people will remember me the better, "he thought. He was not hungry, a crooked knot had stuck his stomach and even the liquor was struggling to get down, yet he had to eat. He got up and went to the toilet, so he would have lost more time, went back to the table rubbing his still wet hands and called the waiter, ordered only one starter saying he would have ordered the rest later, so he would lose even more time.

He ate calmly every serving that came to his table and sipping slowly a white California wine the scented and fruity . He finished the dinner at 11 pm, paid the bill, and went home. He was satisfied, but at the same time a small glimmer of conscience floated in his head and in spite of it he despised himself for what he had done, he was agitated and sweaty, he knew it would be a long night.

***

That evening she had to go to a party, she had lingered more than usual to prepare, in front of the mirror she had tried several clothes combining them with the abundant jewelry she had in the safe, she was not satisfied with the result, at the end she opted for an emerald green dress matched with an emerald necklace and a bracelet of emeralds; The green was highlighted thanks to her blond hair. She completed this with a thread of dark red lipstick and looked into the mirror admiring her work.

The figure in the mirror dazzled and the jewels in the bathroom light sent green reflections. A very interesting young man, whom she had fallen for, was waiting for her. She stepped into the garage and went up to the Mercedes, "My despicable husband is never around when he has to accompany me but this time it is better like this," she thought as she started the engine.

She was over him, he was never present, he did not follow his children, and more than anything he never came to the worldly appointments that she liked so much. His father always said that he was not a man suitable for her but she was stubborn, the more they spoke badly of him the more she insisted. The first months after the wedding were happy, the birth of the two children had gone into the background of the disadvantages that were immediately presented, Many times she wondered if she loved him and whether she'd ever loved him or had been just a whim to go against her father's authority.

She had grown up in wealth always protected by her parents, single daughter, she had enjoyed all the privileges of an easy and agile life; The almost non-existent mother was just a countour of her father. His rise to politics had been tumultuous, he had climbed all the major positions and had become a senator, she liked it but at the same time she did not bear his authoritarian ways, it seemed that everyone should obey him and she rebelled.

She left the garage and took the road that would take her to the party, but just after a few minutes she felt a cold object on her neck and a cold accent-less voice said, "Now don't move and take the first right then Follow the instructions I will give you.

She felt a shiver down her spine. - If It's the money that you want, my husband and my father are very rich but please don't hurt me, - she said in a shaky voice.

- don't talk and do as I tell you - the gun always pressed on the back of the neck caused chills to through her body, the fear made her fragile and an uncontrollable trembling shook her body. They followed the road along the river, rare cars passing in the opposite direction, she thought of stopping the car suddenly and asking for help but they were in open country and did not know what to do. She thought of her children, her father, and even her husband. Soon after the stranger told her to turn to the right, they took a dirty road that continued in the middle of the trees, approaching the river, the road was full of holes and the Mercedes jumped, then the stranger told her to stop, she obeyed.

They felt the flow of the river not far away, a rag dropped under her nose, she leaned, she tried to get rid of it but soon she lost her senses. The stranger moved Barbara's inert body and sat in the drivers' seat. He took the car to the raft, then got down and dropped the car into the river, so the senator's daughter's useless life ended. The killer moved away from the river and took the road back, he had to walk a long way to go back to town, he was satisfied with his job, he put his hands in his pocket and he started whistling.

Mik White was quite happy, an easy and quick job, he did not realize that someone on the river bank had seen everything. Li Sun, like most evenings, had come out to go fishing, at that point of the river there were many catfish and he was fishing dozens, he did so because he liked fishing and because the customers of his Chinese restaurant found them delicious, he had a restaurant at Roseland attended more by his fellow countrymen and less by locals, and catfish made the lion's share of the menu.

That night he had bolted his bike and headed to the river with two plastic buckets attached behind, where he would put the fish he was fishing in. He was already about an hour fishing when he heard the noise of a car arriving. He thought of a couple even

93

though that place was not much crowded, he had watched the whole scene paralyzed by the terror that the killer could see him. After he was gone, he waited for at least ten minutes, then picked up his cellphone and called 911, he had to do his duty as a good American citizen, then took the bike and went after the man.

Chapter 45

He rubbed his eyes looking at the phone on the bedside table, only Sara and Professor Ross knew that number, he brought the phone to his ear.

- Is that you Sara? - He said in a whispered voice.

- It's not Sara - said the voice of a man. - Sara is in our hands and if you want to see her alive again, you have to do exactly as we say.

- Who's speaking? What did you do to her?

- For the moment she is fine but you've done playing hide-and-seek, you have something we want and you have to give it to us, your girlfriend is our assurance that you won't do anything stupid if you want to see her alive.

Alan was silent, his mind was working at a daunting pace, looking for a way out but not seeing it, those individuals were very powerful and well-organized, what could he do?

- All right, what do you want me to do?

- You have to go back to South Bend and come to Sara's place, we'll be there waiting for you, you have to leave immediately, and don't warn the police.

The man closed the communication. Alan was dismayed with the phone in his hand, he must obey; "Poor Sara" he thought "all this is my fault, if she had not followed me now she would be safe."

He dialed Ross's number: Hello Tony, It's Alan, they kidnapped Sara and now they're asking me to go back to South Bend.

On the other side of the phone, Tony Ross remained silent, then said, "You have to obey, I don't see other choice, however, your results are safe, I am studying them, though there is something that does not add up.

- I'm thinking of going to the police.

- Think about it, according to what you told me this are unscrupulous people, I don't want you put in danger Sara's life, you should obey.

Alan left the motel room, got in the car and started moving, "It's going to be a long night" he thought as he hit the main road.

Chapter 46

He was preparing to go to bed when the phone rang, it was Kate

- Chief, they have identified Dr. Adams, they also stopped Rocco Laganà and Dave Patterson and took them to the police station of a nearby town.

- I'll be right down, I'll get dress and be there in no time.

While he pulled on the pants, the phone rang again, it was his wife but he did not answer. "That fucking woman," he thought, "never leaves me alone, but when I'll come back I'll clarify everything ", He went down the staircase to the lobby and stopped at the cafe for a coffee, then headed for the sheriff's office. When he came in, the office looked like a campfire: pizza boxes, beer and cola cans a, Chinese food containers scattered around all the tables, the front wall was full of leaflets and photographs; The map that hung on the wall was full of pins with flags of different color.

- Guys, you're playing here instead of working," he said with joking air but noting the bags under the eyes of all those present.

Even him was not sure in better conditions, the clothes all faded, the frizzy hair that seemed to be pungent and the long beard of two days. Kate updated the special agent about the purchase made by Dr. Adams or Sara Dixon at a motel and the arrest of the two affiliates of Jo's crime family.

"Where are you going, Doctor, whom are you fleeing from? From Jo. But what does Jo want from you, He's devoted to his trades, what can he have in common with you? When I answer this question I will have solved the case, " he thought as he was traveling with Kate to reach the town where they had arrested Rocco Laganà and the other killer. They arrived that was late at night, greeted the agents who had locked the two in the cell and led them into the interrogation room.

- Look who's here, Jo's stupid son, what good wind brings you here?- Pat said, grinning.

- Agent I would like to know why we were stopped, as soon as my father hears about his be sure that your career will endure a good setback, I guarantee it, "Rocco said arrogantly.

- Listen to me, ugly dickhead, - Pat screamed taking him by the collar and raising him at least one palm from the chair where he sat, - *Your* career is already over, actually it never started, and if you don't tell me why you buried that man and why there was all that blood in the car and above all who killed him, I'll send you both in hoosegow and throw the key. I don't give a fuck about that asshole of your father and of those assholes of his attorneys, " he said with the slime to the mouth while splashes of spit splashed in face to Rocco, intimidated.

While he was scolding, Kate entered. - Pat, can you come out a moment I need to talk to you?

They went to the next room where the mirrored glass separated the two rooms.

– They discovered that the fingerprints fund in the house where the old woman was killed Correspond to those of Rocco

Laganà, "said Kate, A mischievous smile was painted on the agent's face.

Pat went back into the interrogation room and sat at the table in front of Rocco without saying a word. After a long silence he began to speak: - Now, you are in the trouble, your fingerprints have been found in Mrs Nora's house, that you have barbarously massacred, I bet you laughed when you slit her throat, but now you will see that there will be nothing to laugh about, you will see that when they send you in a penitentiary, the other detainees will race to break that nice ass you have. You have no escape: either say the truth or I call the prosecutor right away and you go straight to jail, I'll leave you ten minutes to reflect - then he went out. After a few minutes Kate entered the room and sat in the chair.

- Guys, the boss is very pissed and tired, we have enough evidence to send you into jail for a lifetime, if you cooperate perhaps, and I say perhaps You will be able to tear a condemnation from the attenuates. Think about it, your life is at stake - then she stood silently staring at the two men.

Rocco was white in his face and sweating copiously. Dave looked at his hands and tormented his nails, digging under each of them the other hand, then doing the reverse procedure, his head was low and his gaze lost in the void.

- It's better that you talk to me, the boss is not in the best mood, I'm ready to listen to you.

— I want my lawyer, without him I will not say a word," said Rocco, and closed in absolute mutism .The game of the good and the bad cop did not work.

Chapter 47

To reach South Bend he would have to travel all night, and was tired. While driving distracted, he thought of the best strategy. He still had the Glock, he had not yet decided whether to surrender or not. He said he would do it to kill time but did not believe this was the best solution, maybe it would have been better to involve the police, but they accused him of having killed a man, and maybe he did, but not the man they believed, he did not touch him, would they believe him?

If they did not believe him, they would put him in jail and he could not have done anything for Sara, An uncontrollable wrath ascended from his stomach to his brain but his mind kept cold, he would kill those people, now he was certain, he would kill them even in cold blood, He would have been able, he was sure of it. He had always been a quiet guy who avoided jokes and stunts, when he was in Germany many times , it happened to him of having to arrest colleagues who had raised their elbow too much, but, while his companions in turn did not despise to use the truncheon, he had always avoided using violence, preferring persuasion.

Only once, while he was on patrol with a colleague, young and novice, he had come across a soldier cupping himself with cocaine and alcohol and he no longer reasoned, He had tried to convince him but his words seemed to not take hold of him, he offend them, spit on him, and try to kick them. His companion had been paralyzed, also because the soldier was very large, He put all the patience he was capable of, but he did not feel any reason, he did not seem to understand his words, then the soldier advanced and from inside the trousers pulled out a knife, tried before to hit the colleague who was hit in an arm from which came out lots of blood, the novice fainted.

Then he turned to him and tried to hit him. He dodged the first blow, the anger waded and took over, he hit the soldier with a left hook to his jaw that beat his teeth all over, then with a groin he kicked it, he curled into the fetal position and he began to weep With pain, but he did not stop and continued to strike him with kicks and punches, until the calm took the place of the wrath.

He called the ambulance and they took the soldier away, the next day he was called by the base commander who told him that there would be an inquiry, the soldier had reported the fracture of three ribs, jaw and wrist. They said that such violence was not justifiable.

The inquiry commission dismissed him by classifying the act as legitimate defense, provided he gave immediately his resignation. So he returned home, abandoning his military life.

The light of an open bar at night glowed in the distance, he decided to stop to eat and drink coffee. After eating a torpor took over him, he got in the car and decided to take a nap, rest is a weapon.

Chapter 48

Gustavo ran straight away toward Mary and tried to close her mouth, she had awakened from the catatonic state that had wrapped her mind up to that moment, and as if she had been awakened by a terrible nightmare, she was screaming, she emitted screams that of humans had nothing, acute and prolonged. The man put his hand in front, but she bit him so strong that blod came out, then Gustavo resorted to the strong manners and he give to her two slaps, Mary recovered and began to cry.

His wife Gloria came to his mind, when hysterical crises swept her mind, Theirs had been an marriage of love without compromises, they had lived together a happy life together until she was fine, The only bad thing was that their children had not arrived.

Rich of family, he had undertaken a different road than his brothers and sisters, his grandfather Pedro Ortiz, who had emigrated from Spain in the early 1900s, originally from Cadiz, had arrived in America without a penny, had done a lot of work by saving penny after penny. When he had reached a sufficient number, he bought a restaurant. From there his luck had come, from one he had bought two then three until he had created a chain throughout the States. His father, Fernando, and his brothers were no less and had increased and consolidated the chain of restaurants.

Almost all of Gustavo's brothers and sisters worked in catering but he had followed his passion, science. They got married, she was an effervescent girl known in high school and had never separated. After years of common life, one day Gustavo noticed that his wife did not remember things, she had difficulty remembering names of the friends and well-known people. At first it was a mild thing, it seemed to be a forgetfulness of a distracted person, but over time some other symptoms were added, she did not remember where he had put objects, she forgot to cook.

He took her to the best specialists, but each gave a hopeless answer: "His wife is suffering from a galloping form of senile dementia, unfortunately today there are no cures, the situation will always get worse, be there for her.", These were the words that he heard constantly, he felt an impotent anger and a sense of injustice towards the world and all its ugliness. They had everything to be happy, they were rich, he loved his job and they loved each other, they did not have children but they were considering the possibility to adopt one, then tragedy out of the blue.

The situation deteriorated continuously, he had taken a period of expectation to stay close to her, in the last period his wife fell prey to hysterical crises, screaming, tearing her hair, and destroying everything that came under her hand. The first days when these new symptoms appeared, he watched her impotent with tears in his eyes, then he slapped her and realized that the crises were passing, but if at first a puff on her face was enough after a short time he had to give her real and stronger sticks ever.

The situation went on for about a year then he realized that he could not go on doing so and decided to lock the woman in a nursing home. He went every day to see her and was with her all the time. He spoke to her constantly but she did not seem to recognize him anymore, she did not react to any stimulus. Then, after about another six months she died. He had suffered so much but had consoled thinking that his wife would have been better now, wherever she was, what she had lived in recent times could not be considered life. Behind these thoughts and seeing the experience with Gloria he had used the same system with Mary.

- Christ! - said Martin - What inhuman screams, Poor Mary must have suffered a shocking experience, but we'll make them pay for it.

- And how do you plan to do it? - Freddy replied - Those are bandits, unscrupulous people, They don't hesitate to kill, We are scientists, We are not used to fighting.

- We have to go, if they heard Mary's screams they can trace us, - said Gustavo. They walked along the embankment.

Chapter 49

The two men ran as far as the woods would allow, the longer branches slamming on him and some of the more insidious branches in his face, Nathan was ahead and the other behind, They were heading in the direction from which the screams came, they seemed distant. Nathan stopped to breathe again, They remained silent, listening to noises, but everything was silent, the cries were gone, and they felt nothing but crickets and frogs. They went on quickly. When they came to a clearing they looked around, they could have taken any direction, John (or Bill) picked up a piece of cloth in the alley.

- They've gone this way - he said.

They walked quickly by following the path. They had done about two hundred meters in front of them when the lake appeared and, illuminated by the moon, they saw the silhouettes of men walking along the bank. Always without making noise they hurried, When they were just a few meters away, Nathan yelled, "Stop where you are, You have weapons pointed at you, stop there, you have no way out

The scientists stiffened undecided If they were to flee again or obey, they preferred to stop.

"Now I have to tie your hands," Nathan said.

After they tied their wrists behind their backs with some plastic straps, he said, "Which one of you
killed Erwin?

- That pig raped Mary and reduced her to this state, - Martin said.

- It does not matter,- he replied, - you will all end up dead anyway.

They made their way back to the shelter, "Always worse," thought the bad guy.

Chapter 50

Sara came to her senses and opened her eyes, she was tied up and gagged, she was in the dark, lying on a rough and sharp surface, and could not figure out where she was.. The only thing certain was that they had captured her, she had been naive, she should have imagined that they would have waited at her home; Now they would use her to capture Alan. Then she felt the voices weakened and the place where she was held prisoner shuddered, she realized that she was locked in the boot of a car; A door closed and the car set in motion, starting slowly. She felt all the holes the car took, she heard two men but did not understand what they were saying, she did not have much hope to be able to get free but she tried. She was looking for something to cut the twisted ligaments around her wrists, but all the surfaces were smooth, then she decided to try to loosen them by trying to get her hands out, but also this attempt turned out to be vain.

"don't lose your courage," she said to herself, rubbing, at the same time with her hands, the surrounding environment. Then she resigned, there was no chance of escape. She calculated that it was about three hours from when they left, but in those conditions the time was hard to quantify, then the car stopped, the doors opened and closed, heard a distant music.

"They stopped in a pub," she thought, "if I could open the trunk, I would find help," so she played with the look to see if she could open it from inside.

But shortly thereafter, the two men got into the car again. By now, she had all the bones that bore her and her arm had fallen asleep, she started exercising by contracting her muscles in order to resume her circulation, raising the pelvis and inflating the muscles of her arms and legs, then she turned over and began to do the same exercises. She spent a lot of time on the road, she could not quantify the hours, but many of them had passed when the car stopped and the two men came out. The trunk opened and they took her out.

- If you promise me that you will not try to escape, I'll untie you and ungag you, - said one of the men.

She nodded with her head. They untied her and took off the gad as promised, finally she could massage her hands and wrists, she leaned and asked for some water to drink, one of the two men handed her a bottle she was enthusiastically drank. Then they pushed her forward, in a dirt road, she looked around but saw only plowed fields, a remote forest, and a shed in front of them. They were headed there.

Thursday

Chapter 51

He awoke as the sky was beginning to shine, the dawn still could not be seen, but some stripes of reddish light illuminated of reflected light the clouds at the horizon, the air was motionless and the traffic was null. "What a peace" he thought, "if there was not this intrigue in the middle, it would be a day to relax." He left the car to groom, he still had many kilometers ahead of him, the appointment was set for noon and he still did not have a well-defined plan in mind. He did not want to surrender so easily. Considering with whom he had to deal with, once they got the procedure they would not hesitate to kill him and kill all those involved, but at the appointment he had to go.

He took into consideration to call the police, but he kept this possibility as the last resort, He was not sure they would understand, since he was accused of having murdered a man, he did not put much confidence in their intelligence. He checked his gun and wiped it, certainly it would not have served to him a lot, they would have searched him so he could not carry it on him, so what?

With these thoughts he set into motion the car and started at a moderate pace, he could not risk being stopped by some patrol. After a few kilometers he saw the sign of a restaurant that was on and decided to stop for breakfast. He walked into the deserted place where an older maid was cleaning the tables with a rag in one hand and a sponge in the other.

- Is it too early to eat something? He asked.

- Come on in, I just put on the coffee and I can prepare two scrambled eggs, I also have pancakes if you like them.

He asked her everything she had just listed; "Despite all, the appetite does not go away, " he thought. He finished eating, he had drank three cups of coffee and felt well, asked the bill, and before leaving the restaurant he called Professor Ross to let him know about the latest facts and where he was going.

- Are you sure that's the right thing to do? - He asked.

- What alternatives do I have? - He replied. - If I don't go, they'll hurt Sara.

- But if you go you will be captured and they will get what they want.

- I'm aware of this, but I want to end this story, I don't care what they will do with this discovery, I've put in danger both myself and my friends, No discovery, however great, is worth the life of a man, of no man.

- Do as you like but I would go to the police.

- I thought about it Professor Ross, but at the moment I don't think it's the best solution, but if I don't remember wrong in my previous phone call you advised me not to go, take care.

He noticed that despite everything he was in good spirits.

Chapter 52

After having slept, not enough to calm his overdue sleep, he ate a rich breakfast, then FBI Special Agent Pat Blake felt much better and also confident that he could talk to both of them. He had ordered them to be questioned all night without letting them sleep, and without giving them food or drink, he was now anxious to see the result.

The various agents who had succeeded in the task, they had gone to sleep and in the police station, there was only the guard post, two agents and Kate. "Poor Kate" he thought "look in what conditions she is in!"

He took her aside and kindly asked her, - Have they said anything?

- Nothing, - she replied, - Rocco insists on calling an attorney, but he did not say anything.

- Did you warn the prosecutor?

- He'll be here any moment now.

- Now I'm staying and you're going to have a nice sleep, I wait for the prosecutor, I want you perky when you come back - and with a greeting he dismissed the woman.

They brought him a cup of bitter coffee that, as usual, he spat for disgust; the prosecutor, Sam Holligan was a man of integrity, tall, well-dressed and gentle, but inflexible and unsuitable for negotiations. Pat knew about this characteristic and every time he had to work with him he had always struggled to make him accept compromises; but that time he would have to listen to him; If he had interrogated the two with his intransigence he would ruin everything. He still did not get it, he would inform him of the facts and he would kindly ask him to be able to question them. He already imagined what his words would be.

—   You have to hurry, however, if he does not get results within an hour we can't hold him without calling a lawyer.

- I know, - he said, - but I think we have good chances to get them to talk, what can we give them if they speak?"

- Not much but we can avoid life sentence , a sentence of thirty years will be enough.

- I don't think they will accept these conditions, they are convinced that their father's lawyers will be able to get them out as soon as possible and even exonerate them.

- This is to be seen, with the evidence that we have, we hold them in our pocket, and even the father has no escape, of course if they talk is easier, but even if they don't, the evidence are overwhelming. This conversation had taken place dozens of times and he knew this time too.

"Well, I'm going in, I kept them awake all night and they don't seem too fit," he thought, that fucking prosecutor still did not arrive, he opened the door and walked into the interrogation room.

Chapter 53

He had never slept that night, had turned and twisted into the double bed he shared with Barbara, he had risen several times to drink, go to the bathroom, eat something. On the one hand there was his conscience, but on the other, the awareness that all his wife's possessions would be at his disposal, they had made a testament a year earlier and each had named the other heir. With his wife's money he would have had some slack and the things were getting good, they took the girl and the other scientists, and even the doctor was getting ready to "collaborate." As soon as he had the procedure, he would call the military and the things would really have changed.

About five in the morning he had been sleepy and now he slept deeply when a knock at the door woke him up.

- Come in - He said in a sleepy voice.

The butler, Peter, came in, and with an air of regret, he said, "I'm sorry to disturb you, sir, but there is the police at the door and say they have to talk to you urgently for a very serious matter.

- Let them into the living room, I'll be there soon. Meanwhile prepare me a coffee.

He already knew what they wanted, but in spite of this he was apprehensive, the police here meant that they had already found the body of his wife, but so soon?

Then maybe the assassin had not done a good job, he had to go to the police to denounce the disappearance of his wife and show himself broken. It was not expected that the police had already found the body, he was not ready yet. But if it had gone that way, patience. His alibi was perfect, he would have supported the part he had prepared in advance. After dressing he put on his best smile and went into the living room.

- Good morning agents, what can I do for you? He said cheerfully.

The two agents were a man and a woman, both of color and both very young, the man agent said,

- I'm sorry sir, but we have some bad news,- he swallowed the saliva, he saw that he was not yet used to those tasks, - unfortunately this night your wife's car went down in the river ... and she was inside, dead, I'm sorry,- the agent said.

Made an astonished face, opened as much as he could his eyes so as to facilitate the descent of tears, he struggled to make the scene credible and was silent, finally the long-awaited tear came out of his eye. He wiped with the palm of his hand and, with a stuttering voice, said,

- But it is not possible! Are you sure she is? She should have slept at a friend's.

- Unfortunately we are sure, she still had the documents on her, seems that she died around 8.30-9 pm, we don't know how she ended up in the water, she was found in a very isolated area.

He put his hands on his face, and then stood like that for a while, then made a verse that was both a hiccup and a cry of pain.

- My God, poor Barbara, what a terrible end, where is she now?

- She was taken to the morgue, You will have to come with us for official recognition and then she will be subjected to autopsy.

Peter entered with a steaming pot and three cups: - Do you want coffee? He asked.

- I need it, and also something strong.

The two agents refused with a nod of the head, he drank the coffee watered by an abundant dose of brandy and then they left the house.

- I'll follow you with my car.

- No, sir, he must come with us.

They made him sit in the back seat of their car, lowering his head to make him not hit, "Like a criminal ..." he thought.

The obituary was a few miles away from his home, They walked through the wide streets of the city in the middle to the morning traffic of the people who went to work. After twenty minutes they arrived. The coroner's car was parked not far away, the building was a bad construction in reinforced concrete without any painting to make it cheerful, but so both who ended there and those who went for recognition, did not have much desire to cheer.

They entered in a long silent hallway with tall windows that made little light coming in, a row of neon lights lightly lit the floor covered with green linoleum, one of these ceiling lights switched on and off rhythmically making the atmosphere moody; They came to a metal door in front of which was a man with arms folded. They stopped in front of him and the man stretched out his hand and said,

- Detective Donovan, Mr. Davis, I'm the man responsible for the investigation.

He shook the agent's hand and murmured a low. - Nice to meet you

The man led them into a large room full of small refrigerator cells on the walls, on a metal bed in the middle of the room there was the corpse covered with a green cloth. The doctor waiting for them raised the sheet and waited. John was silent trying to get out more tears, but this time he did not succeed, then nodded his head. The officer covered the corpse and then turned to John.

- John Davis You are formally accused of being the murderer of you wife Barbara Andrew You have the right to remain silent. Anything you say can and will be used against you in a court of law. You have the right to have an attorney present during questioning. If you cannot afford an attorney, one will be appointed for you. - after finishing the rite formula the agent took John's wrists and handcuffed them.

- But how? What are you saying? You took a crab, I have an alibi, I was at the restaurant, at least twenty people must have seen me.

- Please follow me, you can explain everything at the station.

- I want to talk to my lawyer right away - he had recovered his natural arrogance, but was frightened, how did they do it?

If they had evidence he was done for. The detective had spoken of a "mandator", the only explanation could be that the police had captured the assassin. He was taken to the police station, he had lost all his security. Two men were waiting for him, one of them being a imposing black with his crumpled nose and a golden tooth buckling when he opened his mouth, the other a insignificant white with a suit blue from the supermarket, big at least one extra size than necessary. The latter made the presentations: "I'm Inspector Bronson and he is the detective Crosby," the man said without stretching his hand.

They made him enter a bare room with a table, four metal chairs and a mirror, invited him to sit and give him a cordless. "Now you can call the lawyer.

His lawyer came after about two hours, went into the room and greeted him with a nod of his head.

- I want to stay alone with my client please, and turn off the microphones, you can't listen to this conversation, - he said authoritatively.

Matt Benson was one of the city's most attentive lawyers, he had an associate firm in which were treated lawsuits in various fields, he cost a fortune but he was worth all the money that he paid for him.

- John, I heard the charges, they are very serious, tell me what happened.

- I don't even know why they brought me to the police station, from what I understand they accuse me of being the instigator of my wife's killing, but I don't know anything about it.

- Listen to me carefully John, they got the assassin and he spoke, the instigator is Jo Laganà who has executed your orders, so don't tell me shit, if you want me to defend you, you have to tell me the truth, so we can choose the most suitable line for your defense, but you have to tell me everything without leaving anything out, do you understand?

John went pale while drops of sweat began to descend from his forehead and behind the ears.

- I need to drink something strong.

- I don't think you are in the condition of asking for a whiskey, at least a glass of water, tell me everything John.

He had his throat dry as a sandpaper, the saliva that tried to swallow did not go down, for the first time he was afraid, all his world was lost, the richness, the fame, the children, the lovers, all. They would lock him in jail and throw the key in a dump, He had many influential friends, he would have gone that way, he would have hired ten lawyers if necessary but had to come out of this mess.

–   Come on John. Tell me everything, - the lawyer urged.

He started to talk, Matt listened to him silently and occasionally furrowed his forehead, then took off his glasses and blew on them and he cleansed them with the appropriate patch, he had reached the point where he had commissioned the murder to Laganà when the lawyer interrupted him.

- Okay John that's enough, I realized you were a stupid and also an impudent, a man in your position who ordered a maimed murder of his wife must have gone out of his mind to do such a stupid thing. We have instead to find a valid reason why you would have been interested in killing your wife.

He thought about it before answering, then began to tell the lawyer all the disadvantages he had with his wife and how she made his life unbearable.

- Let's be clear John, you are guilty, and those things you are telling me are all crap, it's certainly not a good reason to have a wife who likes to participate in social events or who does not want to make love with her husband to kill her

- Of course you are right, but you don't understand how much I was exasperated.

- I can understand, however, How long have we known each other? Twenty, twenty-five? You have always been a bastard., it is true, but me, a wife like the one you chose, I would not want her not even if she was the last woman on earth, so I really understand you, but I'm not justifying you, plus here we are not discussing me and my moral, here we are discussing about you, - said the lawyer.

- What can they do to me? He asked, scared to hear the answer.

- You are lucky that we are in Indiana and there is no the death penalty, otherwise that's what you would have gotten, Here you will get life sentence.

John shuddered at the thought of the prison for life, he could not see himself torn from that beautiful life and locked behind bars indefinitely, he just could not.

- You will condemn John, you have to plead guilty, we must find a motive, the least shameful one and confess that, if you confess that you killed her because she was annoying is the worst thing, if you did it for money, as they suspect, comes right after. We must find a reason or episodes that put your wife in a bad light, Rudeness that she made towards you, if cheated on you, and other things of this tenor, we must not say that you killed her because she had become unpleasant.

A light turned inside John - Of course, why I did not think about it, I have pictures taken from a private investigator in which my wife has sex with another man, I had some suspicions and wanted to check so I hired the investigator.

- Well, this is already a good starting point, passionate crime is certainly seen more indulgent by the juries, especially if you act like a betrayed husband who loved his wife and that at the news of her betrayal, he suffered like a dog.

- And in this case what can we get? He asked.

- If you declare you are Guilty and if we can move the motive from the money to the passion you might get 30 years.

- What? Yelled John - Thirty years? But what the fuck are you saying? And this, in your opinion, would be mild penalty?

- Stay calm, John, the important thing is to avoid life sentence, If you take thirty years and in prison you behave well It may be that you are out in 20.

John listened astonished. - Twenty years is a life, my career, my life, I will lose everything.

- I'm sorry John, really, but I'll tell you something that nobody should ever tell to his client... you could have thought about it before.

The lawyer stood up but he took his arm and forced him to sit down again,

- Have them bring me some water, I have to tell you other things.

He took the glass of water that an agent had brought and brought it to his lips, he drank greedily

- Listen to me now, but carefully, my offenses or wrongdoings or call them as you wish they don't end here. I have to tell you other things that will worsen the situation, you have to contact Jo Laganà and offer him a lot of money to not reveal what I'm about to tell you - and he began to tell him about the scientists.

Once he finished the story, the lawyer looked at him dismayed and murmured: "Fuck! Then he left the room and headed forwards the prosecutor that awaited him with his arms folded and a serious expression in his face.

- Lawyer Benson I don't have much time, I have to run, what has your client decided?

- Mr. Prosecutor, my client pleads guilty and is willing to cooperate.

- Well, I'm surprised, I have to say I did not expect it, but it is better so, believe me, the evidence is overwhelming, shall we go?

Chapter 54

The agent came in the interrogation room, the prosecutor was late, he would start even if he knew perfectly that that was an incorrect procedure. He had rolled up his shirt sleeves up to the biceps, which seemed to burst at any moment. He had loosened the knot of the tie, his long beard and his crumpled nose,. He was sitting down when Kate came in.

- I told you to go rest, Kate.

- I am padded with coffee, I took a shower and I came back, I could not sleep.

- Then gentlemen, as we wait for the procurator let's have a casual conversation , - said Pat.

- I want my lawyer, without him we will not say a word," Rocco replied.

- Okay, in a while you can call him, but let me tell you what you're accused of, then if you want to answer you do it, otherwise we'll call your fucking lawyer,- said Pat, who was getting mad.

- Pat, stay calm," Kate whispered.

-    I'm good and I'm also calm, otherwise I would have caught the neck of these two pieces of shit and I would have turned it like with the chickens.

The two looked at each other in the face without saying anything.

- You are accused of double murder and maybe triple, concealment of the corpse. Pity that there is no gibbet because that's what you deserve, oh how I'd like to see you dangling while kicking your legs and the neck will stretch, and the eyes come out of the orbits, pity, it is a real pity.

Rocco did not resist to the provocation: - And who would we have killed, what evidence do you have to say these things?

–   You are accused of killing Nora Norton, Mik White and Giuseppe Russo, do we need to say that the life sentence is assured?

- Agent you're taking a crab, how can you say we killed these people?

- At Nora's home you've left footprints everywhere, Mik White was killed with a gun similar to yours and you buried the corpse, and Giuseppe Russo with a stone, witnesses saw you - on this point he bluffed, it was not true that there were witnesses. - So if you want to tell me something this is the time, then every thing you will say will be used against you.

The two were sweating and Dave tormented his nails then he carried them to his mouth and bit into one finger at a time. After a long silence, Rocco murmured: - Mik, we did not kill him, he was killed by Dr. Adams.

Pat broke in a loud laugh. - Do you want me to believe that an innocent university professor has killed a man?" This I don't buy it. You tried to blame the doctor for Russo's assassination and now you want to blame him even for that of White, it does not work.

- It's true ,we were chasing them and we were firing at them, He responded to the fire against our car and one of the bullets struck Mik on the neck, he died almost immediately.

- And the other two? Pat added.

- I want my lawyer!

He had fooled him, Pat thought, satisfied. - Kate bring a fucking phone to this stupid guy and let him call the lawyer.

Shortly after, Kate came back with a cordless which she delivered to Rocco.

Laganà's lawyer was a scrawny guy with the hair of a fading yellow and rare, a pair of glasses adorned his face. He walked into the room and put the folder on the table.

- Pleasure, I'm Wilson's lawyer - he said showing his hand to Pat who ignored it. - I would like to speak privately with my clients.

The agents came out of the room and went to have a coffee.

- Sweet, I want it sweet," said Pat, Kate went to the coffee-maker with a smile under the mustache.

Michel Wilson's attorney always served the Laganà family, he knew perfectly Rocco's bullshit and more than once he had pulled him out of trouble. Now Rocco would have to tell him everything, he was always difficult with that boy, he was a liar of indole and a coward, and even when he was telling the truth, he was never the complete truth, but it was more a justification for his actions, or maybe he saw it so , Who knows. He had never understood.

- What happened, Rocco?

- They accuse us of murdering three people, but we only killed two.

- What? Shouted the lawyer. Do they have any evidence? Does your father know that?

- My dad does not know yet, and as the proof the agent says that there are our fingerprints everywhere, but in my opinion it's bullshit, we used gloves, he bluffs, he tries, you know how the cops are, always ready to drop you into the traps.

- We used gloves except when you wanted to drink that tequila from the bottle and you took them off," Dave said for the first time, the lawyer took notes, then looked at them for a long moment and said, "Tell me everything Without neglecting anything.

Pat was eating a donut and drinking coffee with Kate when the procurator arrived all breathless

- Hello Blake, Kate ... - making a nod with his hand. - Can I have a coffee too? This day does not look good, what do we have here?

Pat informed him of the facts and accusations that Rocco and his accomplice were responsible for. The prosecutor listened silently.

- I think that what I heard this morning and this story are closely related, is the lawyer already here?

- It's inside with the clients, - said Kate.

- Well, we'll wait for him to come outside.

As they waited he told them what had happened in the morning.

- So, according to you, Jo Laganà is embroiled in both cases? Asked the agent.

- Let's hear what they tell us, but I think so.

- This time we're really nailing that Mafioso, by the way, let me to talk , you listen, - Pat said suddenly in a good mood.

An agent went to call them saying the lawyer had finished and he was waiting for them. They entered the room in a single row and immediately Pat asked, "Lawyer, are your clients ready to collaborate?"

- They are ready to cooperate but before I want to hear the exact accusations that you are moving to them.

- Well, I don't know all the details of the story, rather I'm curious to hear it from the gentlemen, but I can venture a theory, if I'm mistaken you will correct me. The two gentlemen here were after Dr. Alan Adams, why I still have not figured out and they will explain it to us, they tried to kidnap him several times, but he has always managed to escape from them. The first time they tried at South Bend, and a guy was killed, an Italian affiliate of Rocco's father's gang and they tried to blame the doctor, pity that there are witnesses who have seen them strike with a stone the victim. then they tried to capture him in Prairie City. They dropped their car in the water and killed Mrs. Nora

Norton who had given him hospitality and ultimately they still tried to capture them and, what according to them, the doctor shot and killed their accomplice, They concealed the corpse. that's all, We still don't know why, but the evidence is overwhelming.

A silence full of tension and expectations, descended on the bare room, Rocco sweated copiously and a piece of the lower lip had a trembling, the lawyer stood up.

- My clients declare themselves totally unrelated to the facts that have been notified I will ask for their release.

- Very good lawyer. Take them to jail and put them in isolation, - said, speaking for the first time, the prosecutor.

"What assholes" thought Pat going to the coffee pot. The lawyer came out of the police station very concerned, he had to immediately alert Laganà, it was not only about his son's life, here was at stake the survival of the organization.

Chapter 55

He was getting a massage on his back from his new lover when the phone rang.

- Give it to me please - he said talking to the girl.

He listened in silence and, every word that came to his ear, was a stab to the heart.

- Go away, - he said abruptly to the girl.

She picked up quickly the clothes and slipped away fast; "I'm screwed" he thought, once again he was wrong to trust his son, once again he had made a mess, once again he had abused his patience. He had to save the heritage, he owed him to his daughter, then he would run to South America. He did not know how long was left, but he had to hurry, he went down the street, the driver waiting for him out of the car smoking a cigarette.

- To the bank, quick.

When he reached the bank he ran the long stairs that led to the entrance and opened the door, hurried to the director's office and entered without knocking. The director looked at him surprised.

- Mr. Laganà, what's going on?

- Director you have to help me, I have to withdraw as much cash as possible from my account.

- With so little notice I don't know how much we can give you, If you give me two days I will get you what you need.

- I don't have two days, I don't even have two hours.

- All right, stay calm. Jo, I will call the cashier and will see what can be done - he picked up the phone and talked to the cashier, but while listening his expression changed. - I'm really sorry Jo, your accounts are blocked.

- Fuck! - Laganà yelled and ran outside.

He drove like a fool towards home, in his safe he had some cash, not much but enough for a while, he could not have taken a plane, he had to escape with the car and take refuge in Mexico, but it was far away. maybe it would be better to focus on Canada, it was near and could catch the boat crossing the lake, there they did not ask for the documents.

When he arrived at home he did a sudden stop and went down, leaving the door open, ran in, his wife was not there. "Better so," he thought, he rushed into the studio and opened the large safe. Inside more than banknotes there were documents, he took the only three pack of banknotes that were there, then went to fill a suitcase with few clothes and rushed into the living room, he needed to drink.

The phone rang, he did not want to answer but then he saw it was Rocco.

- You piece of asshole, In what mess have you put me into? He yelled in the handset.

- Dad, they have arrested and accused us of murder," Rocco said softly.

- It's the least, I hope they give you the death penalty so I'll get rid of you once and for all - and he hung up.

"That asshole, I can't believe he is my son? "He rushed down the stairs, had just opened the door when four police cars approached with the sirens on.

Chapter 56

He still did not have a precise plan and he was almost at his destination. He had elaborated several possibilities, but one after the other he discarded all of them, the only chance left for him was to face the men who were waiting for him, But also this plan had many gaps and many unknowns. First of all, it was necessary to see how many men were waiting for him, at least two, and he could take them. But if they had been three or four, the plan would fail, so he was back to square one. He decided, however, that he would improvise. He entered in the city, he still had time, he did not want to arrive in advance, but he did not even have to arrive late. He needed coffee, saw a shop where they knew him and he parked, went into the shop and bought materials that could serve him, then went to the bar to have a coffee.

The day was misty and the sun was glimpsed over the clouds, the air had cooled down compared to the day before and some clouds on the horizon promised rain. Despite the bad day, spring was blossoming in all its strength, He lingered on the veranda of the bar to observe the leafy trees and those with the flowers that were now blossoming, two squirrels run after each other on the branches.

"How beautiful the nature, we can't enjoy it until we are about to lose it, then we regret having ignored it " he thought melancholy.. He got in the car and started to tinker with, he took the gun he had bought in the store and tied it to the calf with the tape, he tried several times the functionality, the gun had to come away easily. He kept the other one in his belt, they would have frisked him and maybe, finding a gun, they would not look for the other, he find that hard to believe, but it was a possibility, Then took the pattada knife and, always with the tape, he made sure to put it under his wrist, He tried several times to get it out of the sleeve, but this was determined at the end he found the solution by making a small cut to the sleeve of the shirt.

He was satisfied with the result even if the knife with the open blade pricked him if he bent his wrist too much. He left again, He would take less than ten minutes to get to Sara's home, he drove very slowly respecting the limits and the traffic lights, a police car came next o him, but after a few blocks the police turned to a side street.

He came to Sara's home and before stopping, he turned around the block several times, turning around and doing different roads, only five minutes to noon. There were no cars in front of the house, When he came back in front there were three minutes to go to the appointment and he decided that it could be enough, He stopped.

Arriving at the door, he was about to knock but it opened and a man appeared, gave a look to the right and to the left then he let him in.

- In front of me, climb the stairs - he ordered.

In the entrance, there was another man with the pointed gun, "And two" he thought. Once inside the second man searched him as he had thought, but he found both guns.

-      Astute, our young doctor. Did you think we would not have looked there? Now you're going to do exactly what we'll tell you, and if you do good, we will not hurt you, but if you do just one joke then we will do it and very, very bad, do we understand it?

So saying, he gave him a fist at his stomach, which made him bend in two, he was prepared for this move and stiffened his stomach muscles, but even taking this precaution hurt him.

Both of them were in front of him and it seemed that there were no other men, he had to try to let them lower the guard.

- what are you going to do to me ? He asked with a resigned air

- You have to follow us, we are going someplace, we'll take you to your girlfriend.

- Is she okay? - He said, always submissively. - You did not hurt her, right?

- She's fine, don't worry, and your friends are fine too, you will have a good reunion.

- Where are we going? He asked.

- You'll see when we're there," replied the first man.

In the meantime they had lowered the guns, the second man had placed it in the holster and the other was about to do so, by now they considered him innocuous.

He only had to decide who was the most dangerous one of the two, at first glance the first man seemed the most determined and the one who commanded, the other seemed like a farmer gussied up , he would hit the most dangerous. It was a good time to act, and he acted.

He slipped the knife from the sleeve and, with a quick move, he stuck it in the throat of the first man, the knife was very sharp and pointed and slipped effortlessly in the man's neck. He threw a cry of pain and fear while a clot of blood spurted. He pulled it off and, before the second man could react, took him by the neck pointing at his throat. The hurt man held his throat crying for help, but the blood gaggled and did not stop, he bent his knees and he fell lying on the floor.

The second man remained petrified, they did not expect a similar reaction of the doctor, they had told them he was harmless, but he was very skilled, on his face passed before surprise then rage and finally fear. The doctor would not hesitate to do with him what he had done with the other.

- What's your name? - Alan asked

- Ramon, - replied the man who actually had the somatic features of a Mexican or South American guy.

- Now you tell me what the plan was and where you were going to bring me, If you don't talk I will kill you. Killing you would not make any difference now.

Ramon spoke, explained that he did not know anything and that they should take him in an abandoned shed to the south of Indianapolis, he did not know anything else, for now it could be enough.

He tied his hands behind his back with tape, Took all the guns and made him go up in the car where he freed him, put him in the driving seat, he sat down behind him.

- Now you take me to that place and don't try to make jokes, you've seen what I'm capable of and I will not hesitate to kill you if you force me.

In reality He did not even know how he had succeeded, maybe it was the anger or the adrenaline, but now that he had realized, He began to wilt.

- No señor, I will not give you any trouble, I have a wife and three children waiting for me, I have nothing against you. Only that the place is far away. It will take long to get there..

- We have all the time we want.

- No señor we don't have all this time, I've heard that they will kill everyone, but I think the others are already dead.

- What the fuck are you saying? Why should they want us dead? I have one thing they want and it is my insurance on my life and that of my friends, you are not fucking with me, right?

- No señor I don't know anything else but I heard this, I'm a poor devil but the man you killed was an important one and he told me these things.

123

Alan was worried. He did not expect this turn and he did not understand why they wanted them dead. Without them and most of all without him the discovery was useless, so why?

Chapter 57

Shoved in by the energizers, she entered the shed, a smell of mold attacked her nostrils, the environment was shabby and drooping.

- Where are you bringing me? She asked mostly to break the tension that pervaded her.

- We're bringing you to your friends, - said one of the two men.

They pushed her toward a corridor and then toward a rusty iron door. The man opened it and the door creaked on the hinges, they pushed her in and closed it. She looked around, there was all Alan's friends, some of whom she knew only of sight, others very well, like Martin.

- Sara, they've taken you too, and where's Alan? - Martin asked apprehensively.

She scrutinized each face, all of them had dull faces except one that seemed to have not suffered any beating, someone had a broken lip and Martin a black eye, all had been subjected to a cruel lesson.

- Martin, I'm fine and Alan should be fine, this until I left him, then I did not have any news. God ... what have they done to you! These men are beasts, but tell me how long have you been prisoners?

- We've been here for three days, we tried to run away but they got us back and they beat us, but it's not as bad as it seems. I'll introduce you to the others, this is Freddy, you already know him, this is Professor Gustavo Ortiz, She is Mary Russel and the man next to me is Professor Tony Ross.

Sara, hearing that name, murmured: "No ...Even you, professor? All our hopes were entrusted in you, now we have no more possibilities, but how did they know about you?

Ross approached her and held out the hand. - Pleased to make your acquaintance, Sara, even if the circumstances are not the best, I'm sorry, I wanted to come to South Bend and they intercepted me near Alan's house.

After the presentations, Sara asked how they had taken them, Each of them told her how they had fallen into the hands of the criminals, then Martin said, - But there is something that does not sound right, we have all been taken, but there is someone who should be here and is not, Professor Gina Wood, she was also part of our "research circle". It may be that she has managed to escape, but I had heard her and she had assured me that she would come, Instead no - Then he told them how he had killed that man and escaped through the woods to the lake and how they had taken them back.

She embraced him tightly, she felt his pain and the repentance of that gesture that was not in his nature. Sara told them about the escape with Alan and how they had miraculously escaped two lurking, at how they had decided to separate to have more chances.

They heard the latch that was turning in the door, five men entered, the tallest held a large tray with food.

- Now eat and then sleep, tomorrow you will have to be in shape, tomorrow comes the boss and you have to answer all the questions that he will ask you.

Martin went on and said, - You're a fool if you think we'll give you the formula, we don't have it, only Alan knows the procedure, we've told you that at least ten times.

The tall man advanced two steps, he put the tray and punched Martin in the stomach who threw the air out of his lungs and bent for pain.

125

- This is what you get when you answer when you're not questioned," said the man, then they all left

When Nathan and the others found themselves in the room, one of the men said,- For me they know nothing, we have beaten them but they have continued to say the same things, if they knew something, they would have said it.

John (or Bill) replied: - Of course they know it, you will see that when we torture them they will speak. Yeah, I just think they'll talk.

"He's the most dangerous, the others are bunglers , but he's really very dangerous, "Nathan thought

- We'll see tomorrow, now it's better to sleep, but one of us has to be of guard outside warehouse, we'll take turns every three hours, who does the first round?

- I will, I am not tired, - said one of the other men.

The night was dripping and the man shuddered in his light jacket, he smoked and looked at the sky, but the stars were not to be seen in that place, so close to the river, In the evening there was always a dense fog which penetrated into the bones and made you shiver. He raised jacket's neck and lit another cigarette, he would have take a walk otherwise he would have fallen asleep.

The frogs were chubby and their kneeling filled the air. Occasionally the concert stopped, and then the crickets froze and tried to overrun the frogs, but none of the animal species ever won. It was two hours now that he was guarding, and soon someone would come take his plase, the air was still and milky, overwritten, even the noises of the animals were now more attenuated.

Suddenly he heard a noise behind a nearby bush, "A fox or a rabbit," he thought, but he held his ears. Nothing, silence, he had also stopped smoking and pulled out the gun. The noise was repeated this time stronger, it did not look like an animal, it seemed to the rustling of someone dragging on the carpone

126

ground. he approached cautiously making a few steps in the direction of the bush always with the gun pointing forward, Even though he was not an emotional type he was intimidated, the noise was repeated this time more attenuated, He had moved, it seemed farther away. Carefully looking alert and her ears tense in the utmost effort to feel the smallest noise, he held his breath and advanced, making sure not to steer the numerous branches scattered on the ground.

Arriving at the edge of the bush, with a sudden move, he leaned forward with the gun ahead, No one, he breathed a sigh of relief, he looked at the night motionless. Then the noise was repeated, this time came from the direction of a huge oak with such a large shaft that it would take five men to embrace it all. Always cautiously he approached the tree, the noise repeated again, the tree was surrounded by shrubs and bushes. Cautiously He came close to the trunk and started to turn around, he came from the opposite side when a noise made him shiver, he tried to turn, but a mighty arm surrounded his neck and a blade was sinking into his flesh, He bent down and tried to contend but the hold was sharp, the blade crossed his throat, he first fell to his knees, then to the ground, holding his neck with his hands in the vain attempt to stop the blood, then his eyes became vitrified and life abandoned him.

Chapter 58

They had put him in the car handcuffed, his protests had been useless, he had also tried to corrupt them, but they did not give up.

He had begun with half a million dollars then got up with his offers, one of them had warned him to quit and to be silent, So he had not opened his mouth any more for the rest of the journey, He had also asked where they were headed because they had entered the state of Indiana, but had not received any response, Then they came to South Bend and dropped him down to the police station.

Two other agents took him and led him to the interrogation lobby.

Here was waiting for him that son of a bitch of the FBI agent Patrick Blake and another man that he did not know, the agent had a smile printed on his face like the expression of a cat preparing to taste a mouse.

- Look who's here!

- Welcome son of a bitch, we finally got you stuffed, you let me spend whole night sleepless to get behind you, but this time you are so fucked ... and your son too.

- don't remind me of Rocco, that's not my son, my wife must have cheated on me, if he was my son would not be like that, - he said angrily. - Anyway I want my attorney otherwise I will not tell you a fuck, and then what do you accuse me of? I did not do anything.

Pat took the phone and handed it over. - Please, call whoever the fuck you like.

Jo called the lawyer, he was in Chicago and he would have taken long to arrive.

- While we wait for the lawyer, do we want to have a chat amongst friends? Pat asked.

- Not a chance.

So they left him alone in the interrogation room and went to have a coffee at one of the offices. While they were seated at the table, Pat asked to the prosecutor: - The story of the scientists you told me from Davis's interrogation, It holds?

- Yeah, The problem is that he does not know where they are held prisoners and if we don't find them I'm afraid we will not find them alive anymore.

- So let's make that asshole talk right away.

- We can't as long as there is no lawyer, I also tried with his son but either he does not know the place or he is more imbecile than what he looks like.

128

- In one way or another we need to know - said Pat.

At that moment Kate came in. - Pat, can I disturb you for a moment?

- What? He asked.

- Sara's credit card was used in a store on the road leading to Bend, very close, the police have already been there and questioned the salesman, he recalls the doctor very well, he knows him personally, he has bought various materials, a gun and ammunition, He seemed cheerful.

- He's coming to Bend," said the prosecutor.

- Doctor come to us if you want to save yourself, - Pat said.

- But why is he coming back? It does not make sense, said the prosecutor pensively.

- No, it does not make sense, something must have happened that we don't know, You don't get to Nebraska just to come all the way back, "he replied.

They stayed there drinking coffee and making guesses until the lawyer came. First they made him aware of the accusations to his client and then made him sit in the interrogation room and told him to hurry up, They returned to their occupation to drink coffee and make guesswork.

The lawyer was very quick, they entered in the room, Laganà had lost all his boldness and held his face with his hands.

- My client is ready to collaborate, - said the lawyer, "but he wants to negotiate a mild punishment, then he will say everything, otherwise he will not say anything.

Pat and the prosecutor looked at each other , and the latter said: your client is not in the position to bargain anything, if he speaks he will have clemency if he does not speak he can expect a life sentence, and already having him clemency costs me a good sacrifice, so I don't want to hear any conditions, on this I don't compromise.

Pat leaned one hand on the prosecutor's arm to invite him to calm then said, "First of all Where are the scientists? Show your

129

good faith to cooperate and I will not promise you anything, hear me well, but I will ensure that you are granted all the mitigating circumstances.

- What scientists? Jo said - I don't know what you're talking about.

- Then you're really an asshole, but an asshole of those who smell, is this your good faith? So you know what? Rot in jail, asshole - Pat had just lost patience, he took the prosecutor for an arm and dragged him out, he was furious.

- Look, why don't you go home, I'll stay here.

- What do you have in mind Pat?

- Nothing special, but I want to try to question him using my methods.

- You know I can't let you do that.

- That's why I tell you to go home, I will not leave a mark on him, don't worry, but if he does not talk those people are dead.

Shaking his head the prosecutor left not too convinced, soon after even the lawyer left the room.

- Lawyer, you are a reasonable person, please convince your client to cooperate, it's all over anyway.

- I've tried it, believe me, I've recommended it in all the ways, he says about his son but he's worse, he is more stubborn, sorry agent, goodbye.

Left alone he dismissed the other agents with an excuse, took a baton and, knocking it on one hand, entered the room.

Chapter 59

On the way, they had talked so much and Alan had believed that Ramon was really a good poor devil who had been looking for a job and he ended up in the wrong place, So, without lowering the guard, he had invited him to tell him everything he knew, at first he was reluctant to talk, then he gradually opened up.

- Señor, if you take that gun away from my neck I swear on my mother that I tell it all.

Alan thought he could try to trust him and then took the gun away from the neck of the bad guy but did not put it down, he laid it on his knees, always holding it.

The Mexican continued. - I don't know many things, I only know the place where the other people take prisoners, I also know that those people were kidnapped by Jo Laganà, and his son, on the order of a very rich man, but you don't ask me the name because I don't know. What I heard was that they were happy with this deal and they would make a lot of money, Me and two other left and we arrived at the shed, We gave it a clean up and equipped a room with beds and another with beds, food and a video surveillance system, then we went back.

- And who they were the other two? Alan asked.

- They're two who work with the gang, but they are two small fish, we only do the job of maneuvering, we don't deal with anything else, I swear I've never hurt anyone.

They continued the trip and, suddenly, Ramon had become very talkative , He talked about his wife and children and how he ended up in the gang, about how he had illegally entered the States and about the mother-in-law who lived with them. Half-way into the trip they were almost friends, they took the state road 94 and then took the 65th, after a while Ramon saw a grill.

- Señor Alan can we stop to eat something? I have not eaten anything since last night. Alan agreed, he also needed some more coffee and he was hungry.

According to Ramon they would arrived at the shed at night and it was good to get into strength.

- All right, let's stop, but remember I always keep you under the gun, so don't do anything stupid otherwise I would not hesitate to shoot you.

- don't worry señor, I will not do anything.

131

They entered in the bar, not very busy, they ate in silence, Alan looked around but he did not notice anything suspicious.

—   If you help me then I'll help you," Alan said to the Mexican, now he trusted him enough, he realized he was not a violent person, but only a poor man who tried to make ends meet.

- Señor trust me, I never liked those people, with weapons I'm not good, but I can shoot it a gun- Ramon replied.

Alan went to pay with the credit card, then they resumed their trip.

Chapter 60

The special agent left the interrogation room with the baton in his hand, A grateful smile crumpled his lips, The care had made the hopeful effect, only that Laganà did not know where the scientists were kept prisoners, That only Rocco knew, Pat was sure he had told him the truth, with all the hits he had given him. He had not left any signs on Jo but he was almost sure he had pain everywhere, only that this complicated things, the time was tight and he had to find them before his men killed them, if they had taken the doctor then there would be no more escape.

With these thoughts in mind he went to the coffee machine, he really needed it, he met Kate with a paper in his hand.

- They found the doctor in a grill on Indianapolis Road no more than half an hour ago,- she said, handing the paper to him.

"Indianapolis? But why so far away? Could the refuge be there? "He thought as he rolled the paper into his hands.

- Listen to me, Now I'm going to question Rocco, You warn the Indianapolis Police, then organizes the S.W.A.T. So as soon as I come back we'll also leave.

- But we don't even know in which car he travels, how do we find him?

- Rocco will tell me, this time, even if I resign, he will tell me – and so saying he turned to take the baton and headed for the exit.

Chapter 61

The scientists ate in silence the pigswill which had propelled them, Sara's eyes were fixed on the plate and with the spoon she carried the food to her lips, She had the fixed look and was reflecting on the situation and on the discovery that the five assisted by Professor Ross were working on, She was a math teacher and she did not understand well the quantum formulas She did not even understand Schrödinger's theory. She had a rational mind and that was not much rational she could not understand how a phenomenon could be defined as "Undefined", for her, a mathematical formula, if applied to some factors, must always have the same result independently by the factors that were applied, but obviously it was not.

As soon as she had finished eating She turned to the other fellow prisoners. - Can someone explain to me, in very poor words, what were you working and what were the results?

The others looked at her and, Martin spoke first - It's not easy to explain what we did, You need to have some concepts of quantum physics and quantum mechanics and explain it in poor words is not easy for me.

- At least you can try, then if I don't understand at least I'll know what you are talking about," she said, she could not tolerate it when they underestimated her brain.

Freddy said, - I'll try to explain it to you. You must know that when Schrödinger formulated his theory, also Einstein laughed at him together with other scientists; it Was the year 1953 and together with Boris Podolsky and Nathan Rosen he formulated the paradox EPR from the initials of the three scientists but they were wrong. Later on another scientist, an Austrian physician named Zeilinger, has demonstrated the accuracy of the theory and here comes the phenomenon of the entanglement, which is one of the properties of quantum mechanics, have you ever heard of this phenomenon?

- I don't think that I have ever heard of it, - she said.

- To make a practical example, without a doubt, you will have heard of the feelings that the homozygous twins feel, in some cases, what one does feels the other does too, a pain, a displease or joy and happiness proven by one are also reflected in the other. This happens at any distance the two people are, we could say that the twins are in constant contact wherever they are, this too can be called an entanglement. This is called quantum correlation, since it can't be reproduced individually but only as overlapping of two systems, so there is a distance correlation between the two entities, For example, we take two quantum-related interconnected particles, If one of them is suffering a variation of any type, the other one will instantly have the same variation at any distance. Quantum entanglement is the basis of quantum computers and of the possible quantum teleportation.

- But where did you arrive? Ross asked. - I looked at the material that Alan sent me and those formulas don't seem to work, or rather they seem incomplete.

- You're right, Professor, actually we were at a dead point, We could not reproduce the phenomenon, but maybe Alan did it, But you don't ask me how and why, I don't know, "Freddy added.

- Do you understand now, Sara?

- Partly yes, So do you tell me that Alan might have reproduced the entanglement in a lab?

- It may be that he succeeded - said Martin, - but only he can tell us.

Chapter 62

They entered a dirty road that ran between the high bushes, on the right side there was a forest, while the left side were only fields.

- Señor, we don't have to get to the shed otherwise they will hear us, I take the side road that approaches the river, we can leave the car and walk closer.

- All right, take that road.

- If you trust me you should give me the gun, I don't know how many are inside, but with two guns it's better.

Alan thought about it for a moment, then decided he could trust him but he wanted to be cautious: - Okay, when we get near the shed I'll give you the gun, but now turn off the headlights otherwise they can see us from this distance too.

The side street was disconnected, full of holes where the car could be snagged, Ramon was driving cautiously trying to avoid them, but when it came in with the wheels, the car was struggling to get out, They continued slowly for about a kilometer then stopped in a clearing, protected by trees, They went to the shed.

The path was studded with trees, not very dense but very large, they hid behind a trunk, They were listening and then, down and running, they tried to get to the next trunk that would have them covered. The night was drizzling and the fog filled the surrounding environment, as they moved, the crickets stopped singing and then resume undeterred as soon as the two intruders had passed.

Suddenly the shed stood in front of them wrapped in fog, from inside came a dim light, On their side the ground was uncovered, while moving more to the right, the wood almost came to skim the building. They moved to the right always keeping the posture down, approaching the river, there the fog was thicker than ever and the shed sometimes disappeared from their view. They came a few meters away from the metal structure, "And now what do we do?" He thought, trying to work out a plan. The reality was that he had never had a plan, he had confided to making a decision once he came to the place, but now he did not know what to do.

Whispering he handed the gun at Ramon: - And now?

The Mexican looked at him with his small eyes and then said, "We don't know how many there are and we can't face them all together, We have to hope that some of them come out to smoke a cigarette in the open air and then we take him down, but without making noise, then we see.

For Alan it seemed the only thing to do and always cautiously he walked to the front of the shed where there was the entrance.

Chapter 63

- That asshole of Tom must have fallen asleep, Peter go see where he's gone, - said John (or Bill).

Peter, who was eating a burger, said he would finish the sandwich and then he would go

- Right away for fuck's sake, He had to be here an hour ago

Sadly Peter came out of the room to look for the accomplice

- I'm leaving too, I have to stretch my legs, this damp air is getting inside the bones, I'llgo to the bathroom and then I'll go outside, - said John / Bill heading to the bathroom.

Nathan was alone with another accomplice, He did not even know his name or he had forgotten it, his brain worked frantically, he was desperately trying to find a solution but had to wait for a good opportunity, This could be good but not great, he had to wait again. Peter came out in the night with the flashlight in front of him, but with all the fog he could not see more than two meters away, He was obliged to hold the torch turned to the ground so that it did not reflect on the fog wall, blinding him. He started to call, heading toward the small group of trees but, from the accomplice , no reply.

"He can't have fallen asleep, He would hear me, "he thought Increasingly circumspect and cautious, He advanced slowly and, occasionally, called him; He pulled the gun out of the holster, he did not like that situation at all. When it became clear that his friend would not answer, he fell on his knees while listening to the noises of the night.

To his right , a rust broke the silence, He turned slowly toward that direction, listening, He began to be afraid, even if he was a tough guy, as he defined himself, He had always been involved in group actions but, to be face to face with the danger made him physically sick, He started sweating copiously and one step after another he headed to the point where he heard the noise.

Suddenly a louder noise made him jump, sending his heart in his throat. This noise came to the right of the previous one as if a person was moving cautiously. He headed for the new direction always with the ears tense and the sweat that flowed from his armpits and back; he arrived at a very large bush and he hid, He no longer felt anything, maybe a nocturnal animal wandered from those parts ... but the friend, where was he?

He decided to go around the bush, always with his pointed gun which preceded him, he advanced in small steps trying not to make noise, then he saw the legs coming out of the bush and he was sure there was no nocturnal animal, He bent down to see if the friend was still alive but the light of the torch illuminated a puddle of blood: they had killed him

The teeth began to move by themselves with an uncontrollable beat, the shout of an owl made him jump, making his heartbeat run and he almost dropped the gun out of his hands. He still took a couple of meters when something hard fell on his head, splitting his skull, the last thought he had in his mind was to give the alarm but the cry he wanted to throw died in his throat, bubbling a set of catarrh and blood, he bent his knees and fell to the ground.

Chapter 64

The S.W.A.T. team decided that the best solution was to go up the river, The two black rafts with men on board, Along with Pat and Kate walked silent the river. The men of the special team wore all trousers and were dressed in black, they had the night watchers around the neck and were all in radio connection, including the two FBI agents, with earphones in the ears.

Three of those men had the precision rifles with shoulder strap, with telescopic mirrors and laser pointers, the inflatable boats were equipped with an electric motor, and apart from the lapping of the water on the hulls, They did not produce any noise. "If the police always cooperated with the FBI, things would be better, much better," Pat thought.

By now the objective was close, according to the indications he had gotten from Rocco, He had to struggle less than expected to make him speak, as soon as he had told him that his father was in jail and Davis had been arrested, Rocco had felt defenseless and all the arrogance he had manifested until that moment had disappeared as of enchantment, he felt no more untouchable.

He confessed everything, First he told him where they could find the corpse of Gina Wood, Then he gave the directions to reach the place where scientists were kept prisoners, these were very precise. He confessed all he had committed, He justified by saying that his father had been ordering him to do everything and that he had only obeyed the orders, that coward had started to shake like a kid and he had not to use the bullet, which he had taken along and had put in a good display on the table that separated him from the bandit.

As soon as he had all the information, He started off quickly, scraping the tires of the car, calling Kate and reporting everything to her, giving her the necessary orders. Now they were running across the river, hoping to arrive in time to avoid a massacre.

It started to rain, At the beginning, a few drops barely perceptible that were confused with the splash of the inflatable, Then more and more intensely until becoming a real storm, A strong wind rose to dissolve the fog, The stabs of the water droplets that crashed on her face hurt. The wind strengthened with angry gusts and then settled down almost completely, then began to blow more forcefully.

The inflatables brought near the shore downwind to shelter, at least in part, from the storm that had begun, They had the opposite wind and the electric motors were struggling to navigate against the current.

"Damn it, This is bad" He thought, trying to get down and lower his jacket, but his stature did not help him, the men had the overalls but he had gone in a jacket and tie, just like Kate was dressed in light clothes, fortunately they were almost there.

- How long will we be on the target - he shouted to be heard above the wind and rain at the command of men, The man looked at a GPS detector and replied that it would take about twenty minutes under those conditions. Resigned he tried to get as much shelter as he could, but now he was drenched and pissed.

Chapter 65

He had hit hard, too much. The stone he had used as a weapon sunk in the skull of the man, He did not want to kill, but had not been measured his force. In that stroke he had put all the repressed anger of those days and he had clearly heard the occipital bone break with a crack, blood, mixed with gray matter, had remained in his hand leaking, he had cleaned it on his pants. Meanwhile It had started to rain in a consistent way, while a strong wind had swept away the fog.

The tops of the trees swayed, some more subtle tree almost touching the ground with the top, he was going to call Ramon when a voice made him freeze.

- Stop where you are, bastard, don't move or I'll blow your brains out - Then he felt the cold barrel of a gun leaning on his neck. - Finally we got you, you killed two of my men, but I'll make you pay ... oh you'll pay dearly! You and that slut of your girlfriend, I'll have a world of fun, and I assure you that you will suffer a lot before dying, you will see, you will beg me to shoot you, and now walk.

John / Bill had come out to stretch his legs, he was walking when he had seen the whole scene, he was hiding and tried to approach without being seen when a man suddenly turned from behind the bush with a stone in his hand and had Hit Peter; Then protected by the wind and the rain, he had walked towards the doctor and stopped him.

Finally, they had captured him, but the doctor had done too much damage, to be a doctor he was a tuff guy, but now they had caught him, they would have him talk and then they would have killed him.

Ramon was hiding behind the big oak tree trunk where he had thrown the stones to produce the noise, but when he realized the man who was reaching behind the doctor was already too late, he Had thought to shoot him but could hit Alan, so he was confined to being hidden. he would follow the two men and then decide what to do, Certainly he could even leave, no one had seen him, but he had given his word and his word still had a value, He would try to help him hoping that, if everything would resolved well, the doctor would help him.

John / Bill pushed Alan into the shed and called the other companions: - Come, soon, I caught that bastard of the doctor, he killed my men, but now he's fucked.

- You can't touch him until he will have talked - Nathan intervened.

- You'll see that he'll talk right away, wait until I submit him to my care and you will see how much he'll say.

He opened the iron door and pushed him in. - Wait for me, I'll come back soon,- then he closed the door. Sara saw him and she ran to meet him, embracing and tightening him tight while tears of joy went down her face.

- My God you are safe, what did they do to you? Are you ok? What happened to you?

He put a hand on her mouth and stroked her hair - I'm fine, for now they have not done anything to me - he looked around. - Professor Ross, did they take you too? How did they do it?

Ross burst into laughter. - Hello Alan, they have not caught me at all, I would say that if everybody was caught, the merit is mine.

Alan looked at him with a surprised expression in his face, even the others looked at each other without saying a word, they were all amazed at that news.

- But how? What do you mean, Professor?

Ross, quietly, continued: "Look Alan, every time you call me to ask for advice and tell me where you were I told everything to them, In fact as soon as you informed me of what you had discovered I warned John Davis and he got in motion.

- But, for God's sake, why? I thought we were friends, you were my teacher, you taught me everything I know.

- Alan, you don't understand that he is a bastard and he wants to take credit for your discovery? Sara exclaimed.

- Your girlfriend is smarter than you, apparently, "Ross said. - See, you've discovered something that could revolutionize the world as we know it now, and how did you do it? By chance or luck, not by reason, I've spent my whole life researching, neglecting my free time, my family, and what did I get from this? I tell you, nothing. A poor retirement, no recognition, I no longer have a family, I have nothing, no one has ever considered my publications, no one knows me, it's not right. so when this opportunity came to me, I immediately realized the potentialities and I decided that I should be the one who had discovered the phenomenon, I had to take the merit not you or them, - he said, pointing to the scientists who were astonished listening to him with open mouth.

- The rancor does not make you think, professor, how could you have thought such a thing? There have been many dead people already and they are all on you, - Sara said.

Alan was literally astonished, the professor was a person to admire, he was grateful for his brilliant mind, for his genius intuitions, and now he had revealed who he really was, a weird and rude individual. He was not better than those bad guys, or perhaps he was worse than them, At least they had devoted their life to a crime by choice or because they were forced by circumstances, such as Ramon, but they knew they hurt people. someone had scruples others no, But him, his idol, he would never believe he was capable of doing a wicked act. Instead he had done the worst action of all, he had betrayed his confidence for a discovery, for the fame he would derive from it, to satisfy his ego.

Alan did not know whether to be angry, outraged or just disappointed, Ross continued his delirious speech. - But you did not tell me the whole truth, right? - You've been hiding something because those formulas don't work, at least those you've given me.

- If you are so good and so capable you should immediately locate the missing part, Instead you are a fool, you say I have had luck but it is not true, I got there trying and trying again, and even though I still don't understand how it works, I'll get it.

142

You have really disappointed me, Professor, I really liked you and instead you have revealed to yourself as a despicable man, unscrupulous individual, ready to hurt to achieve your goals, I tell you, you disgusting me, - Alan said.

- Anyway, you'll tell me what I want to know.

- You don't hope for it , what you want to know I don't know, The formulas are the ones I sent you, - said Alan, bluffing.

- I don't believe you, In those formulas you missed something, you don't trick me, but you will see that my friends will make you talk, then all of you will have to die and finally I will be famous, I will have what I have always deserved and never had.

A wild anger hit Martin, the indignation was blowing his mind and, to those words, he completely lost his mind, with a leap he reached Ross.

- You, son of a bitch - and began to strike him with terrifying hits, the peaceful bear had become a lion and was now crushing his victim. He beat him with two consecutive punches in the stomach, which were terrible, then began to hit his chin and nose. Ross was a man who was not very muscular and was not used to the fights, hence he was subjected to aggression without reacting. Martin continued to strike more and more violently.

- Stop, stop! - Gustavo screamed. - You're killing him, stop Martin, don't be like him," he ran towards the two who, clinging, were rolling on the floor.

Alan, still surprised, watched the scene paralyzed, even Freddy was unable to move, Sara screamed. Nathan who had listened to the whole conversation opened precipitously the door and catapulted inside, took Martin's neck with a Mata Leao grip, but he did not let go. When the air was almost gone, Martin loosened his grip.

- Let me go bastard, leave me!

The other two men, hearing the hustle they were catapulted inside, John / Bill and the other man pulled out the pistols and,

143

holding everyone under the gunshot, John / Bill screamed: Now stop, Stop doing the ruckus, Nathan leave that bastard to me - and so saying, he took Martin by one arm and fired at his knee, For his luck the shot did not go to full mark but chipped the bone and the bullet came out. For him the pain was tremendous, he slumped, holding his knees with both hands and yelling.

- You,- he said, turned to Alan, - now you come with us, - and he took him by the arm always with the flat gun. - Try and revive the professor, we have to bring him with us.

Nathan and the other man took Ross and dragged him, fainted, out of the room. They brought Alan and the professor to another empty room, where only a strong light illuminated the screeched walls, the only furniture was a metal chair where they tied Alan with plastic straps.

- Now let's see if you talk," said John, then turned to Nathan, - Try to revive the Professor, we need him to be conscious.

Chapter 66

When they arrived, he was, by now, dripping wet up to the marrow, the strong wind and the rain covered their noises, the team S.W.A.T. Put in safety the inflatable boats and then, in a single line and with the night-watchers around the head, they walked, with low head, towards the shed.

The commander told one of the agents to go first, covering him from the possible enemy fire and then, one at a time, the others reached the position of the first, Pat and Kate closed the line.

On earbuds, the commander's voice resounded. - Shooters be ready but don't shoot if not behind my order, we must try to save the hostages, we don't know how many men we have against - Each one confirmed the order received.

They were now at the main entrance, cautiously one of the agents peered inside with the viewer, it was all dark and no one was visible. A light green glow came out of the door of a corridor; Always in a single line covering each other, they went into the wide room heading toward the light.

The corridor trailed down to the right and to the left, to the left, right at the bottom, there was a light from below a door, to the right there were two more doors, even these posing at the bottom, facing each other. One of them was open and the light turned on, from the closed one filtered a little light, and from there came a chatter.

Two officers went to the left to check, the others went to the other side where noises came. The two agents who had gone to the left said, whispering, that the door was closed with a latch and a padlock ,Inside people were moving.

- don't do anything, Stay there, we don't know where the scientists are.

Then a scream came from the closed room to the right. The agents went to the front of the door.

- Ready to raid, - said the commander.

The door had only one handle that kept it closed, Cautiously the captain tried to lower it, it was silent, the other agents were in position, ready for any event.

- On the count of three,- the captain said softly. - One, two ... three, - he lowered the handle and opened the door. - Stay where you are, - Intimated the commander..

There were five men in the room, one tied to a chair with what it looked like a paperclip planted in one arm, Another was on the ground lying down and seemed senseless, The most massive man who was already behind the man tied repaired himself, lowering and putting his gun at the temple, Another of the men threw himself to the ground and the other pulled out the gun, ready to fire.

A series of bullets crossed his body when the agents fired at the same time, the man fell to the ground, shot to death.

- don't take another step or I'll blow his brains out - said the man behind the prisoner. The other man was not far away and was covered by a metal table.

- You have no where to go, you are surrounded, don't worsen your situation if you want to get out alive,- said the commander.

- Throw your weapons to the ground and get out, otherwise I'll kill him, - he shouted.

The air was full of tension, The situation was stalled, Suddenly Nathan, who was on the ground, fired two gunshots, One of them hit the bandit's head and he rapidly took cover but he was not fast enough, the agents started shooting, Nathan shouted, "Stop, stop I am a DEA special agent, don't shoot!

The shots hit him on the arm, leg and abdomen.

- Throw the weapon and come out of there," said the commander.

Nathan came out as much as possible with his hands raised but he could not to stay standing, Before fainting He managed to say: - In my pocket there is a leaflet with a phone number, call it, they will confirm my identity.

Finally Pat could relax, That criminal would end up in jail and he would remain there for a long time followed by that idiot son of his, The organization was now dismantled and even that other fisherman of John Davis would not come out for a long time, Things had ended the best of ways, Certainly if there was not that infiltrated DEA It would have been more difficult. His intervention had been providential. Now his priority was to go home and sleep a whole day, that is if his wife would permit it. He picked up the phone and called, This time he was determined to take that vacation and bring his son fishing.

Epilogue

The organ sounded slowly the Mozart's Requiem, Alan with his arm worn tied to the neck was moved, Sara at his side was absorbed in a prayer, the other friends with their heads lowered listened to the melody that drifted from the cane of the organ and reached every corner of the church, Martin was on a wheelchair, a lonely tear descending on Mary's cheek.

The coffin of the light colored wood in front of the altar was covered with flowers that emanated an intense scent. Gina Wood's family cried softly.

After the melody was over, the priest blessed the coffin and sprinkled it with incense reciting the Eternal Rest. those present recited subheading the formula. Then the scientists lifted the casket and took it to the funeral wagon waiting outside. Everyone followed it to the cemetery. Each of them threw a handful of dirt on the coffin that was now in the pit. Sara laid a rose..

Two days after the function, Alan and Sara were enjoying lunch from Parisi's.

- Tonight we have a meeting at my house, are you coming? Said Alan.

- Yes, I will love to - she replied.

The spring left room to the summer and in the air there were the typical odors of June, the days had stretched and the sunsets had fluttered, the warm air around them gave a sense of serenity; They were not yet well aware of the dangers they had undergone, but they were resuming their normal life. That evening they should have decided what to do about their discovery. each of them had returned to their family, at least who had one, and the others to their solitude.

Professor Ross was battered but alive from the Martin's claws, he was in the infirmary of the prison waiting to be judged for what he had done. Mary had recovered from the terrible experience, but the violence she suffered would permanently mark her and she'd never be like before, Alan and Sara spent all the time together.

They walked out of the restaurant, holding hands, and headed for the park, which was only a few hundred meters away. they were silent and smelled the smells of the surrounding plants and the bright colors of that sunny afternoon, they sat on a bench in the shadow of a majestic oak and Alan lit one of his beloved Tuscan cigars.

That evening they all arrived on time, ordered pizzas and beers for dinner, they ate evoking the facts just happened. After dinner they moved into the living room where Alan offered them an aged scotch. Then Alan stood in front of the computer.

- Now I'll explain the formula I applied and I had missed to put in USB I send to Ross, I don't even know why I did this, but at that moment I felt like doing it - then he began to snatch formulas and parameters.

The friends nodded except Sara who did not understand anything of all those diagrams. After the presentation Martin spoke: - What do we do now?

Ortiz, who had listened in silence, said, - My God, this is a shocking discovery, it will allow for developments that are hard to imagine.

- Are we sure this is what we want? - Freddy replied - If we publish the discovery, life on the planet will be revolutionized, but is humanity ready for it? Even today we can't live in peace between us, wars in the name of religion, economic wars, a part of the world, in this case the minority of people, has most of the wealth, the other party that is the majority is still starving. We are not a united race devoted to the common good, but a mass of individuals where everyone thinks of their own personal gain

148

not caring of others, if our neighbor has different skin color from ours, we still look at him with suspicion, I don't think we are ready for this.

They discussed animatedly, everyone said their opinion but they did not find an agreement, there were those who wanted to exploit the discovery, who wanted to make it public and free to use and who instead wanted to destroy it. At midnight they still had not reached an agreement, in particular Ortiz wanted to continue developing the project while Freddy wanted to destroy it.

Then Sara intervened. - I don't understand anything about those formulas, even if it's something I should understand since I graduated in mathematics, but I understand what it might serve. I say my opinion even if I have nothing to do with you. It is a shame not to carry it forward, but I agree with Freddy that humanity is not yet ready, just see what happened and it's easy to imagine what would happen if you should tell the world about the discovery. Those individuals are not the only ones who would kill to get it, I would say that the best solution is to develop it secretly, without making it known, then when it's over, deposited it at a notary and decide what to do with it later on.

Everyone looked at her.

- It seems a reasonable solution, - said Alan, the others agreed that this was all right, they would continue to develop the project because it had become their reason for life, but they would keep it a secret.

They did not realize however that their discovery was now known to the military. One by one the South Bend scientists came out of Alan's house, He and Sara headed toward their bedroom.

The next morning they had to go to college, lessons were almost over and those would be the last of the season. They came out of the house, the insects where everywhere in the air,

149

the air was scented with violets and the wisteria that they had near the veranda spread an inebriating scent, they reached the pavilion where they held the lessons, and after they saluted each other, they separated to reach their respective classroom.

Alan turned to the left, he had to take a long corridor, his room was at the end, in the hallway there was a man who was sweeping wearing a cap. He approached, lifted the strained of his hat and said, "Good morning, Dr. Adam, good day today!

- Good morning Ramon, you are right it really is a nice day.

END

NOTES

Between fiction and reality.

The characters of this book are all fantasy, while the places where the facts are taken are all real and reflect the features described in the novel.

The implications of the scientific aspects narrated in the history, although fictional, have an affinity with the reality, in fact quantum entanglement or quantum correlation is truly one of Erwin Schrödinger's revolutionary theories.

These theories were initially not welcomed by the scientists of the time, including Einstein himself, who expressed many perplexities, to use an euphemism, about such theories. Subsequently, in 1998, the Austrian scientist Zeilinger and other scientists have confirmed the results according to the theories that are at the base, in particular quantum transport is not part the writer's imagination but one of the many possibilities that open up on the horizon of quantum mechanics. Here are some of the experiments conducted by the Austrian scientist, as an example. Below are the experiments that are still being studied by Anton Zieilinger (Wikipedia source), as long as you can read them without getting a headache.

Neutron interferometry

As a member of the group of his thesis supervisor, Helmut Rauch, at the Vienna Technical University, Zeilinger has participated in many neutron interferometry experiments at the Laut-Langevin Institute (ILL) in Grenoble. The first of these experiments immediately confirmed a fundamental prediction of quantum mechanics, the change of sign in a spin phase due to a 360 ° rotation. This was followed by the first experimental implementation of a coherent overlay of spin of matter waves.

He continued his work in neutron interferometry at MIT with Clifford G. Shull (Nobel Prize in Physics in 1955), focusing in particular on dynamic neutron diffraction effects in perfect crystals, due to overlapping coherent to more waves. After returning to Europe, he produced a very cold neutron interferometer that anticipated subsequent experiments with atoms. These experiments included a more precise test of the linearity of quantum mechanics and a double slit experiment with a single neutron at a time in the apparatus. In reality, in that experiment, while the arrival of a neutron was recorded, the next neutron still resided in the nucleus of uranium, waiting for the fission to take place.

Quantum entanglement

By the end of the 80s, Zeilinger was interested in quantum entanglement. This work has produced its most important results and opened the new field of quantum transport, quantum computer science and quantum encryption.

Along with Daniel Greenberger and Michael Horne, Zeilinger wrote the first absolute article on quantum entanglement with more than two particles. The resulting theorem, called GHZ, was fundamental for the quantum physics because it provides the more succinct contradiction between the principle of location and the predictions of quantum mechanics. In addition, GHZ states are the first example of entanglement or many particles that have never been investigated. These states have become essential in quantum information. GHZ states are now also a PACS code entry.

As a professor at the University of Innsbruck, Zeilinger began experiments on photons in entangled states. His purpose, from the early nineties onwards, to demonstrate the GHZ contradiction, was finally succeeded in 1998.

Along this path, Zeilinger has developed many new tools for physics of entangled photons, for example a strong source of entangled photons compared to polarization, techniques for identifying Bell states and methods for producing the coherent emission of more than a couple entangled by a crystal. The resulting technology allowed him to run a number of first quantum information experiments with entangled photons. The first absolute use of the entanglement in any quantum information protocol was the demonstration of hyperdense code.

His achievements include the first encryption based on entanglement, the first quantum transportation of an independent photon, the first realization of exchange of entanglement and the experiment that closes the vicious circle of communication in a test of Bell's inequalities.

Since 2000, Zeilinger's research has focused on quantum computation completely based on optics, development of quantum encryption system based on the entanglement, and experiments with photon pairs entangled on long distances. In optics-based quantum computational experiments, Zeilinger and his group were the first to demonstrate a number of basic procedures such as purification of entanglement and particular quantum gates. This culminated in the first quantum computation demonstration one way, including more recently active ultra-fast control. The one-way quantum calculation scheme was used to realize Grover's search algorithm and various quantum games, including the prisoner's dilemma.

In quantum encryption, the Zeilinger group is developing a prototype in collaboration with the industry. While most of the community was working on a much simpler scheme with the use of weak laser pulses, Zeilinger based its approach exclusively on the most complicated scheme using entangled photons. A recent demonstration that entanglement is a necessary condition for the security of the quantum channel confirms the correctness of this choice.

Zeilinger experiments on the distribution of entanglement on large distances has begun both with free space and fiber optic communication and transport between laboratories located on opposite places of the Danube River. This was extended to larger distances through the city of Vienna and, in 2012, up to 147 km between two of the Canary Islands, beating the measure established only a few days before by a Chinese team and paving the way for quantum communication with satellites . His dream was to bounce light entangled by satellites in orbit. He has succeeded with an experiment in Italy with the Matera Laser Ranging Observatory.

An important and fundamental relapse of these experiments was the first test in 2007 of a non-local realistic theory proposed by Anthony James Leggett that goes significantly beyond Bell's theorem. While Bell demonstrated that a theory that is at the same time local and realistic is in contradiction to quantum mechanics, Leggett considered various non-local realistic theories in which one assumes that individual photons carry polarization. The resulting inequality has been shown to be violated in the experiments of the Zeilinger group.

Conclusions

If you have read until this point and you understand all that has been explained in the Wikipedia text (which I doubt) maybe teleportation is not so science fiction as it might seem at first glance.

Youcanprint
Finito di stampare nel mese di aprile 2019